"I'd like to make love to you. Very, very much," Jonas stated.

"Em, there's no need for you to look like you're being asked to commit for life here. We're old enough to know we can take pleasure where we find it."

"And walk away afterward?"

"That's right."

"Except it doesn't work like that," Em told him sadly. "Like me and Robby."

"I don't understand," Jonas said.

"I thought I could just love Robby for a little bit, so I let myself become involved. And the longer it goes on, the more it'll tear my heart out when he leaves."

"You could adopt Robby."

"Oh, yes?" she jeered. "How could I do that when I'm on call twenty-four hours a day, seven days a week. What sort of mother would I make?"

"I think you'd make a fine one."

Families in the making!

In the orphanage of a small Australian seaside town
called Bay Beach there are little children desperately
in need of love. Some of them have no parents,
some are simply unwanted—but each child dreams
about having their own family someday....

The answer to their dreams can also be found in
Bay Beach! Couples who are destined for each other—
even if they don't know it yet—are brought together by love
for these tiny children. Can they find true love
themselves—and finally become a real family?

Previous books in the PARENTS WANTED miniseries
by RITA nominated author Marion Lennox
in Harlequin Romance®:

A Child in Need (#3650)
Their Baby Bargain (#3662)
Adopted: Twins! (#3694)

THE DOCTORS' BABY
Marion Lennox

PARENTS
WANTED

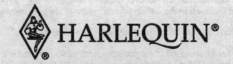

HARLEQUIN®

TORONTO • NEW YORK • LONDON
AMSTERDAM • PARIS • SYDNEY • HAMBURG
STOCKHOLM • ATHENS • TOKYO • MILAN • MADRID
PRAGUE • WARSAW • BUDAPEST • AUCKLAND

This book is dedicated to all women with breast cancer
whose past involvement in research and clinical trials
has so improved our chances of survival today.

ISBN 0-373-03702-3

THE DOCTORS' BABY

First North American Publication 2002.

Copyright © 2002 by Marion Lennox.

CHAPTER ONE

DR. EMILY MAINWARING had been awake all night, delivering twins. She was probably asleep and dreaming, but right in her waiting room was...

Her ideal man!

But... This *was* Bay Beach. She *was* in the middle of morning surgery, and staring was hardly professional. Instant marriage wasn't on the cards either. So somehow she forced herself back to being a twenty-nine-year-old country doctor instead of a lovesick teenager staring at a total stranger.

'Mrs Robin?'

The elderly Mrs Robin rose with relief. She'd been waiting far too long. Every other patient looked at her with envy, and the stranger looked up as well.

Whew! He was even more good-looking eye to eye, and when their gazes locked...

For a moment, Em allowed herself to keep looking. Doctor assessing potential patient.

Ha! There was nothing professional in the way she was looking at this man.

For a start, he was large, in a strong-boned, muscular, six-feet-of-virile-male sort of way. Then he had the most gorgeous, burnt-red hair, crinkling into curls that were a bit unruly, and made you just want to run your fingers...

'That's enough of that! Concentrate on work!' she told herself sharply. The last thing she needed this morning was distraction, and if a pair of twinkling green eyes had

5

the capacity to knock her sideways then maybe she was even more tired than she'd thought.

'I'm very sorry,' she told the rest of the waiting room, the stranger included. 'But I've had a couple of emergencies. I'm running almost an hour late. If anyone would like to sit on the beach and come back in a while...'

It wasn't likely. These people were farmers or fishermen, and a visit to the doctor was a social occasion. They'd sit placidly enough, outwardly reading magazines but in reality soaking up every piece of gossip they could get.

Such as who the redhead was.

And she might have known they'd find out.

'He's Anna Lunn's big brother,' Mrs Robin told her before she even started on her litany of ills. 'He's three years older than Anna, and his name's Jonas. Ooh, isn't he lovely? When he came in with Anna, I thought maybe she had a new fella, and that wouldn't hurt at all since that no-good Kevin walked out. But if this can't be her new man, then it's good that she has a brother kind enough to bring her to the doctor's, don't you think?'

Yes. It was. Anna Lunn was barely thirty, yet already weighed down with poverty and kids. But why...Em glanced down her list and saw the appointment, and she couldn't suppress her misgivings.

Anna had made a special appointment and she'd brought her brother along for support. Em just knew this wasn't going to be a five-minute consultation for a pap smear.

But there was little point in worrying about it now. With an inward sigh she mentally added another half-hour to her day and turned her attention to Mrs Robin's blood pressure.

                    *   *   *

Charlie Henderson collapsed before she'd finished. Booked in for his regular coronary check, the fisherman was so old that he looked shrivelled and preserved for ever. He'd tucked himself into a corner of the waiting room and had been contentedly observing the kids and chaos and general confusion. Now, just as Em started writing Mrs Robins's prescription, his eyes rolled in his head, he crumpled and slid soundlessly onto the floor.

'Em!' Her receptionist was banging on Em's door before he hit the carpet, and Em was by his side almost as fast.

The old man was deathly white, cold and clammy. Em did a fast check of his airway and found no obstruction.

And she found no pulse.

'Get the crash cart,' she snapped at Amy. She gave Charlie four deep breaths and ripped his shirt wide to bare his chest. There was no time for niceties here. and there was no time to move him. This looked like total cardiac arrest.

And Amy wasn't her usual receptionist. Lou was off sick. Amy was standing in and, at eighteen, she had no medical training at all.

Em was on her own.

She could only try, and she must try now. To attempt resuscitation with all these people watching was dreadful, but there was no time for anything else.

'Could you clear the room?' she demanded between breaths, not looking up from what she was doing, and not even hopeful that anybody would listen. She couldn't care. She was breathing for her old friend, pumping down on his chest in an attempt at cardiopulmonary resuscitation as she waited for the crash cart.

And then, from above…

'Could you all move outside? Now!' It was a male voice, backing up her order with harsh authority.

Em blinked, wondering who the voice belonged to. It was rich and deep and seemed accustomed to command, but she was kneeling on the floor beside the old man and her attention was totally with him.

Breathe... Please, Charlie, breathe...

'As you see, this is an emergency and we need room to work,' the voice continued. 'If your need's not urgent, can you make an appointment later. Otherwise wait outside. Now!'

And then suddenly, magically, Red-Hair was kneeling on the other side of Charlie. The crash cart was beside them and she had someone placing jelly on the paddles as if he'd done it countless times before. As she rolled Charlie onto his back, he helped adjust him—just as if he knew what he was doing.

Who on earth was he?

There was no time to ask. All she could do was move with him, fitting a proper mouthpiece now the trolley was here. Normally she wouldn't have tried to breathe into a patient without a mouthpiece, but Charlie was special. Charlie was her friend.

Charlie...

She had to stay professional. There was no room for emotion if they were to save the old man's life. With the mouthpiece fitted, she gave him four more quick breaths, then the deep voice cut in.

'Move back. Now.'

He shifted away. She did too, and then it was the stranger's hands that fitted the paddles over Charlie's bare chest. He knew exactly what he was doing, and she could only be thankful.

Please...

The charge hit and Charlie's body jerked in convulsion. Nothing. They both stared at the trace. It showed no heart activity at all.

They must keep trying! Em gave him four more deep breaths. Then...

'Back again.'

The stranger's hands brought the paddles down once more. A jerk—yet still the trace showed nothing.

She breathed for the old man again. Over and over. Still nothing.

And finally Em sat back on her heels and closed her eyes. 'Enough,' she whispered. 'He's gone.'

There was absolute silence.

Amy, standing behind them in white-faced horror, drew in her breath and started to cry, her tears streaming silently down her face. She was too young for this, Em thought wearily. And, aged all of twenty-nine, Em felt suddenly far too old. She rose stiffly to her feet and crossed to give her receptionist a hug.

'Come on, Amy. This is OK. Charlie wouldn't have wanted it any other way.'

That, at least, was the truth. Charlie lived and breathed for Bay Beach gossip. He was eighty-nine, he'd known he'd had a dicky heart for years, and to go out dramatically in the doctor's waiting room, rather than by himself at home, was just the sort of ending he'd think fitting.

'Ring Sarah Bond, Amy,' Em said wearily, as Amy sniffed and tried to pull herself together. 'Sarah's Charlie's niece. Tell her what's happened. She won't be too surprised. And then could you ring the undertaker?'

Finally she took a deep breath and looked up at the man who'd been helping her.

'Thank you,' she said simply, and something in her face must have betrayed her exhaustion and emotion because the man swore softly. He crossed the distance dividing them to stand before her, and placed a pair of strong, male hands on her shoulders.

'Hell. You're done in.'

'N-not quite.'

'You were fond of Charlie?'

'Yes,' she said. 'Everyone's fond of Charlie. He's been a Bay Beach fisherman all his life.' She looked uncertainly down at Charlie's body. They'd closed his eyes, his body had gone limp and he looked incredibly peaceful. Asleep. This was death as it should be.

She shouldn't mourn, but... 'I've known him for ever,' she whispered. 'He taught me to fish when I was five years old. He taught me to swim and he taught me...so much else. So much about the ocean and about enjoying what I had. So much about life.' With that, her rigid control broke, and her voice broke with it.

'You need time to recover.' He looked outside where there were still half a dozen patients who'd decided they were urgent enough to wait. He could see that as soon as Em had spoken to Charlie's niece and the undertaker had taken Charlie away, this overworked doctor had yet more work to do. 'Do you have anyone else to take over?'

That reached her. Em took a deep breath and fought for resumption of normality.

'No.'

'Then I will,' he told her calmly. 'I'm a surgeon. This sort of medicine may be unfamiliar territory, but I can cope with urgent cases while you get your breath back.'

'You're a surgeon?' Her voice was incredulous. She knew he must have medical training—the full implications just hadn't sunk home until now. 'Anna Lunn's brother is a surgeon?'

Anna didn't have a cent to her name. This wasn't making sense.

'I'm a surgeon all the time,' he told her. 'I'm only Anna Lunn's brother when I'm allowed to be.' He gave a short, harsh laugh, and then pushed away whatever it was that bothered him. 'But my problems can wait. I can certainly see your patients and deal with anything urgent. Let's get Charlie sent off with dignity, and then take time for a cup of coffee. The only thing is…'

'Yes?'

He hesitated. 'It's taken me weeks to bully my sister to come and see you,' he said, and the reluctance to give her more work was plainly written on his face. 'We had to leave her children in emergency child care at the Bay Beach Homes while she came to see you. It's almost been like a military operation to get her here, and if I let her go home now I won't get her back. Will you see her?'

'Of course I will.'

'There's no "of course" about it,' he said. 'If you do, it's on the condition that I look after your urgent cases after that.'

'There's no need.'

'There is a need.'

He looked at her more closely then, and Em wondered just what he was seeing. She was pale at the best of times, tall, over-thin from skipping too many meals or eating on the run, and her slimness was accentuated by her long dark hair braided down her back.

Normally braiding her hair back from her face suited her, but she was aware that fatigue had created shadows under her brown eyes and made her finely boned face look etched with strain. Her colourful print dress, one of several that she wore almost as her uniform, now only accentuated her pallor.

And, yes, he could see her exhaustion. His next words confirmed it. 'Don't you have any help at all?' he asked explosively, and she spread her hands in a negative.

'Why the hell not?' he demanded. 'Surely Bay Beach is big enough for two doctors—or even three?'

'I was born here and I love it,' she said simply. 'But there are lots of lovely little coastal towns in Australia for doctors to choose from, and most of them aren't as far from the city as this. Doctors want restaurants and private schools and universities for their children. We've been advertising since my last partner left two years ago. We haven't had a single response.'

'So you're it.'

'I'm it.'

'Hell.'

'It's not so bad.' She ran a hand over the smooth silkiness of her braid and sighed as she looked down at Charlie. 'Except sometimes. Except now. I'm so glad you were here—so I know that there was nothing else that could have been done to save my friend.'

'I can see that.' He, too, looked down at Charlie's limp body. 'Damn.'

'It was time for him to die,' she said softly.

'Like it's time for you to go to sleep.'

'Nope.' Another weary sigh. Then Em pulled herself together, and her usually laughing eyes managed a smile. 'There's no rest for the wicked, Dr Lunn,' she told him. 'Or should that be Mr Lunn?'

'Make that Jonas.'

Jonas…

It sounded nice, she thought. Right. 'OK, Jonas,' she agreed. The undertaker was pulling up outside. 'Let's say our goodbyes to Charlie and then I'll get on with my morning's work.'

'You heard what I said,' he growled. 'You see my sister, and then I'll take over until you've had a rest.'

The temptation was almost overwhelming. She had two patients in hospital who she really should be with now. If she left Dr Lunn—Jonas—with the surgery, she could see them, have breakfast-cum-lunch and maybe even have a nap before afternoon clinic.

'Do it,' he said, and she could hardly resist. Heavens!

But to hand over her work to a stranger was totally irresponsible.

'I'm fully qualified,' he told her, sensing her last qualm. 'A quick phone call to Sydney Central will confirm it. I promise.'

She believed him and it was good to resist any further. 'It sounds wonderful,' she admitted. 'You're on. But, first, let's see your sister.'

'She won't tell me what the trouble is, but she's scared stiff.'

Half an hour later Em was back by her desk. What had happened seemed unreal. But before her sat Anna Lunn, pale-faced and silent. Gripping her hand, as if willing strength into her, Jonas looked almost as grim.

'I don't know what's going on, Dr Mainwaring,' he told Em, and she cast him a quick glance. He'd turned formal. It was a good idea. This had to be purely professional.

'Anna doesn't let me close. She and I went our different ways early, and she's never let me help her, even though bringing up her kids on her own must be a nightmare. But now... I came down to see her a couple of weeks ago, and something's scaring her. She won't tell me what. But I know her well enough to realise it's something bad. I've been badgering her by phone from Sydney ever since. Finally I've made her to agree to come and see you.'

'Anna?' Em turned her full attention onto the woman before her.

Like her brother, Anna was a vivid redhead, but there the resemblance ended. Younger than her brother, she actually looked much older than him. Her short red curls were a bit uneven, as if they'd been cut at home, her green eyes were shadowed and she seemed...defeated.

In fact, she looked as if the world had dealt her some really hard knocks, and with this one she was about to topple over.

'Y-yes?' Her voice was barely a whisper, but Em could hear the fear.

'Would you like your brother to leave so you can tell me what's wrong in private?' Em cast a warning glance at Jonas. Having brought her this far, he must understand he had to be prepared to back off.

But he knew. 'I'll go if you like,' he offered, and half rose, but Anna's hand came out and caught him.

'No.'

Jonas sank again. 'Then tell us what's wrong, Anna,' he said softly. 'We're with you all the way. Both of us are. But you have to tell us what's happening.'

Anna took a deep breath. She raised her face to Em's and her eyes were like those of a rabbit caught in headlights—terrified beyond belief.

'Tell us, Anna,' Em said gently, and the girl shuddered.

'I don't...I don't know if I can face it. My kids...'

'Just tell us.'

'There's a lump in my breast. I think I have breast cancer.'

There was, indeed, a lump in Anna's breast. It was as big as a pea and close to the nipple, and it moved a little as Em gently palpated it.

'How long have you been able to feel it?' Em asked,

carefully examining the rest of the breast. There was nothing else—just the one tiny, single lump.

'F-four weeks.'

'Is that all? That's great,' Em said warmly. She had Anna on the examination couch behind the screen. Jonas stayed out of the way, but he was still within earshot. 'It's very small and you've come early.'

'Early?'

'Some women worry about a lump like this for a year or more without having it checked,' Em told her. 'You have no idea the kind of trouble that can cause. But you've come quickly. And this is small. It's less than a centimetre across, I'd think,' she added for the benefit of the listening Jonas.

But Anna was trembling under her hands, afraid to meet her eyes. 'So it is cancer?'

'It might well be a small breast cancer,' Em admitted. There was no use giving false reassurance when the most important thing was to get Anna to agree to have the necessary tests. 'But there's also a very good chance it's just a harmless cyst. Cysts in breasts are common—much more common than cancer—and they feel very similar. It needs a biopsy to tell the difference.'

'So...' The girl's eyes flew to hers, hope flaring. 'This may well be just a waste of time. If it's just a cyst, I can go home and forget it.'

'Yes, but you can't go home and forget it yet,' Em told her. 'Because you may be right in your first guess. Your age means that you're in a low-risk group for breast cancer, but we have to exclude that possibility.'

'But I don't want to know.' Anna put her hand to her mouth as if to stifle a sob. 'If it is...cancer...then I want to be as normal as I can for as long as I can. I have three kids. I want to be there for them. Jonas made me come, but if it's cancer then it's better not to know.'

'Well, that's exactly where you're wrong.' Em handed Anna back her blouse—and a tissue—and waited until she was decent. Then she pushed back the screen so Jonas could join in the conversation. 'It's far, far better to know.'

'Why? So you can cut off my breast?'

'That hardly ever happens any more,' Jonas growled. Unable to restrain himself, he rose and moved to give his sister a hug. 'For heaven's sake…Stoopid. Why didn't you tell me? I could have eased your fears.'

'By agreeing I may have cancer?' She was looking wildly from one to another. She was very close to the edge, Em thought, and knew this visit was the culmination of weeks without sleeping. 'No one's easing my fears now.'

'I can do that,' Em said gently, but there was a note of iron in her voice. What Anna didn't need was false sympathy or reassurance. She needed facts. 'Sit down, Anna.'

And Anna sat, still looking like a hunted animal. She was like a tigress defending her cubs, Em thought, and suddenly realised that the comparison was appropriate. Anna wasn't scared for herself as much as for the three small children who depended on her.

'Anna, your brother's a surgeon,' she told her, casting a quick glance at Jonas. He could intervene any time he liked, but she sensed he wanted this to come from her. 'He'll back up everything I say, but I want you to listen.'

She held up her hand.

'One, you've come very early, and the lump I'm feeling seems very well defined. That means it's either a nice little cyst, which we can confirm with a biopsy, or, at worst, it'll be a small cancer that we can remove. Now, I can't make promises until the tests have been done, but if, as I suspect, it's confined to the one small area, then there'll be no question of you losing your breast, even if it is cancer.'

'But I'd want...' Anna gasped, then continued. 'If it's cancer I'd want it off. All off. The whole breast.'

'Surgeons don't remove breasts without very good reason,' Em told her. 'Even if it is cancer, with modern surgical techniques there's usually no need. They'd simply take away the affected part. That means you'd be left with a scar and one breast a little smaller than the other.'

'And that's it?' Anna looked as if she just plain didn't believe Em. 'What about chemotherapy?'

'If it's as early as I suspect it must be, then you'd undergo a six-week course of radiotherapy just to mop up any stray cells. Then you and the oncologist would decide whether you wanted chemo.'

'But...'

'The survival rate for early breast cancer is great,' Em said firmly. 'After surgery and radiotherapy it's well over ninety percent. And it's not the fearful experience it once was. Honestly, Anna, about the worst side effect of current chemotherapy is fatigue as your body copes with medication, and hair loss. And hair loss is no big deal.'

She grinned. She may as well be honest here. 'You and your brother are so good-looking that having shiny scalps would only make the pair of you even more attractive. It'd just bring you back to be on a level with the rest of us ordinary mortals.'

'And I'd shave with you,' Jonas said promptly, and he finally succeeded in drawing a smile from his sister.

'You wouldn't.'

'Watch me!'

Em blinked. The thought of a bald Jonas...

Good grief. Once more, there was a wave of pure fantasy. Jonas bald…

She was right. They'd both be stunningly attractive, no matter what they did to their hair, or…or anything.

But Anna was back on consequences. 'I don't want to be bald.'

'So you never need to be,' Em told her. 'The health system in this country makes sure you'll get a wig if you want one, no matter what your income is, and wigs are great.' She smiled at the pair of them. The tension was decreasing by the minute. 'You know June Mathews?'

'I…yes.' Everyone knew June. She ran the local minimart. June was a stunning strawberry blonde. Or, to put it more truthfully, she was an interim strawberry blonde. Until she tired of it.

'June doesn't dye her hair.' Em's smile widened. 'Whenever June tires of her hairstyle, she just buys a new one.'

'You're kidding!'

'I'm not kidding.' Once more, Em's voice gentled. 'She doesn't mind me telling people who need to know, as long as I ask that you don't tell anyone else. June suffers from alopecia—hair loss—and she's been wearing a wig for twenty years.'

'I don't believe it!' This was clearly a side of June that stunned Anna, temporarily diverting her from more serious issues. Which was just what Em wanted.

'Believe it. And I know there's nothing June would rather do than help you choose a wig if it ever becomes necessary. She adores wig-buying. She told me once that choosing hair is better fun even than sex!'

Then, as Anna blinked in astonishment, Em pushed home her advantage. She smiled her most reassuring smile. 'But, Anna, we're crossing way too many bridges, and we're crossing them way too fast. As I said, chances are we're talking about a cyst.'

'You'll be fine, Anna,' Jonas added, and Em heard the catch of emotion in his voice. This was his baby sister after all.

Em looked at Jonas and she realised with a sense of shock that he, too, was asking for reassurance. For facts! As a surgeon, he must know the statistics, but he wanted to hear them out loud.

Cancer was a frightening word, she thought, no matter who faced it, and the only way to lessen the fear was to confront it head on.

Help me, he was asking, and it was suddenly all Em could do not to put out a hand and touch his. Her smile died.

Because brother and sister were both afraid of one thing. Anna was taking a long, drawn-out breath, searching for courage for the next question.

'If…if it's cancer, it'll come back,' she said finally, and her voice was now strangely calm. 'I'll die. My kids… Sam and Matt and Ruby. Ruby's only four. Who'll look after them?'

'Anna, I've spent the last twenty-four hours giving piggy-backs to your three terrors,' Jonas said, in a tone of one much maligned. 'I love your kids dearly and of course I'd take care of them, but for the sake of my aching back, can we arrange to have you live?'

'I…'

'Please, Anna.'

Anna took another deep breath. 'I don't have a choice, really. Do I?'

'We don't,' Jonas said. He rose and his hands clenched and unclenched. He'd also been under a huge amount of strain, Em realised, wondering just what was wrong with his sister. This must come almost as a relief. There were so many worse diagnoses than early breast cancer. 'Anna, I love your kids but, let's face it, they'd be much better off with their mum than with their Uncle Jonas.'

He grinned then, a wide, lazy grin that sent Em's insides doing crazy things again. Stupid things! She had to force herself to focus on what he was saying.

'I'm willing to stay in Bay Beach while you need me,' he was telling Anna. 'In fact, I have a feeling that Dr Mainwaring could use some help, too, and with two women in need, what's a man to do but stay?' He flashed them another grin, even wider than the first. 'So can we organise these tests and get on with it, please?'

Anna looked up, long and hard, at her brother—and then she turned to Em. In her face was a slackening of terror. There was still fear, but less. The hardest decision had been made.

And the smile she finally gave almost matched her brother's. 'Yes, please,' she said.

'Then let's do it.' Em reached for the phone and started dialling.

CHAPTER TWO

EM WOKE to afternoon sunlight.

The feeling was so novel that for a moment she thought she must be dreaming. Then the morning's events came flooding back, and with them came emotions so complex she had trouble taking them all in.

First there was Charlie's death. Despite his age, there was a sensation of emptiness and grief which she needed time to absorb.

Em tried hard to stay dispassionate but, as the only doctor in a small country town it was impossible. And she'd known Charlie all her life. Em's parents had died when she was tiny. She'd been raised by her grandfather, and Grandpa and Charlie had been close mates.

With Charlie's death had gone one of her last links to her childhood—to memories of weekends fishing in Grandpa's old tub of a boat, or sitting on the pier baiting hooks while the two men yarned in the sun—or having them make her endless cups of tea as she'd studied her medical texts while they'd gossiped easily over her head.

She'd loved them both. Grandpa had died two years ago, and now Charlie had gone to join him.

She'd miss Charlie so much.

And now there was Jonas…

She was so muddled in her thoughts. She'd lain down for a few minutes and two hours later she was waking to confusion—the intermingling sadness of Charlie's death, the tension of the lump in Anna's breast…

And the thought of Jonas.

Why did he keep overriding everything else? He was just *there*, a lightening of the dreariness of her awful day, and the sensation was so novel that she let it dwell.

Well, she let it dwell for all of thirty seconds. Then she rose, rinsed her face, gave her mirror a good talking-to for being lax enough to allow another doctor—about whom she knew nothing—to take over her duties.

She needed to check on him, she told herself. She needed to know who this man was. She might instinctively believe him, but she was trusting him with her patients and the medical board would look pretty darkly at someone who just stood aside and let a quack take over their duties.

And one phone call was all it took, to a long-time friend who was an anaesthetist at Sydney Central.

'You have Jonas Lunn working for you?' Dominic's voice from the staffroom at the Sydney hospital was an incredulous squeak. 'Em, the man is brilliant. Brilliant! He's been offered a plum teaching job overseas and the powers that be here are already wondering how we can fill his shoes. He's the best—as well as being one of the most caring professionals I've ever worked with!'

Now, how had she known he'd say that?

'You hang on to him,' Dominic said seriously. 'Em, if he's offering to help, you take all the help you can get.'

Hmm. Maybe. He was only here for the day, she told herself.

So with a struggle she hauled her muddled thoughts into order and sallied forth to once again become Bay Beach's sole doctor.

But she was no longer sole doctor. Jonas wasn't giving the position up lightly.

'Go home,' he growled as she opened the surgery door and peeped in. 'I'm busy.'

He was, too. Young Lucy Belcombe, nine years old and accustomed to lurching from one catastrophe to another, was now suffering from a greenstick fracture of the forearm. Jonas had the X-ray up on the screen so Em could see at a glance what was happening. Jonas was applying a last layer of plaster as Lucy's mother watched, and Mrs Belcombe was obviously deeply impressed that such a splendid-looking male was taking care of her daughter.

These people don't even know for sure Jonas is a doctor, Em thought in a little indignation.

He was, though. He looked up at her and he smiled, and Dominic's words were confirmed. The impression he gave was of pure competence. 'We're doing really well without you, Dr Mainwaring,' he told her. 'Aren't we, Lucy?'

And Lucy agreed. 'Dr Lunn told me I was the bravest kid in Bay Beach when he gave me the needle,' Lucy told her proudly. Then she gave a sheepish grin. 'And he also said I was the dopiest.'

'Hmm.' Em looked again at the X-ray. Lucy had certainly done her arm some damage, though she'd been lucky in that it was just a greenstick fracture. 'Treeclimbing?' she guessed.

'A really big one out on Illing's Bluff,' Lucy admitted, not without pride, and Em winced.

'Oh, Lucy. If you climb then you're supposed to hang on. I guess Dr Lunn's not far wrong when he says it was stupid.'

'Yeah, it was a bit dopey.' Lucy gave her a rather white-faced smile and then looked sideways at her mum, as if wondering whether she should admit the next bit. 'It won me five bucks, though, 'cos it was a bet and I got to the top.'

'And did you get an extra payment for coming down the fast way?' Em demanded, and Jonas chuckled.

He had the nicest chuckle, she thought. Sort of deep and resonant and infectious. It made you want to smile just to hear it.

'The very fastest way,' he told Em, still chuckling. 'Lucy's just lucky she didn't land on her head. Will you deduct the five dollars from the clothes she's torn, Mrs Belcombe?'

But Mary Belcombe just gave him a reluctant smile and shook her head. Lucy was the youngest of her six daredevil kids. Broken bones were part of her lifestyle.

'I'm good at patching,' she said simply. 'I have to be.'

'And so are we.' Jonas gave the arm one last long look, tied a sling around it and popped the plastered arm inside. 'Right. One patched arm. I want to check it again tomorrow to make sure I've allowed enough for swelling. Meanwhile, if it starts hurting much more than it is now, give us a ring.'

'Give me a ring,' Em butted in, and got a sideways grin from Jonas for her pains.

'Scared I'm doing you out of a job, Dr Mainwaring?'

'You can have all of my job that you like,' she told him, and the smile died.

'Yeah. There's certainly a heap of it. Far too much for one person.'

'One person is all there is,' she told him, and ruffled Lucy's hair. 'Goodbye, Lucy. Take care.'

'Care isn't in her vocabulary,' his mother said bitterly, ushering her daughter out the door. 'Thank you, Dr Lunn.' And then she turned to Em and added in a conspiratorial whisper that Jonas couldn't help but hear, 'Oh, my dear, he's gorgeous. I'd hang onto him if I were you.'

And she left, with Em blushing from ear to ear.

'I've left detailed notes on everyone I've seen, if you'd like to review them. With the Belcombes gone, Jonas gave her an efficient summary of the last two hours. Mrs Crawford's the only one of any real concern, and that's mainly because of her diabetes. She's had intermittent vomiting for two days. I don't think it's anything major— she says she ate some fish she thinks was off—but she's starting to look dehydrated and her blood sugar's up. So Amy and I admitted her.'

'You and Amy admitted her?' Jonas's businesslike tone was designed to bring her down to earth, but in truth it did the opposite. To have someone take over was such a novel experience it practically took her breath away. 'You *what*?'

'Amy and I admitted her,' Jonas said, and his eyes twinkled. 'With the help of your nursing staff. I've put up a drip and left her on hourly obs. Not a tricky concept, Dr Mainwaring.'

'But strange,' she threw back at him. 'No one admits anyone to hospital around here except me.'

'Welcome to the new order, then,' he told her, and watched with interest while her eyebrows hit the roof.

'I beg your pardon?'

'Wouldn't you like a new partner—temporarily?'

She could only stare, and the laughter lines in his broad face creased further. 'Close your mouth,' he told her kindly. 'You'll collect flies. And do stop looking like I've slapped you across the face with a wet fish. I'm only asking for a job.'

'Asking for a job?'

'A temporary one,' he told her kindly, as if she were

just a little bit stupid. 'I need it.' He still smiled, but his look softened as if he understood just what his offer meant. As if he knew just how exhausted she really was. 'Sit,' he told her calmly, and, shocked into submission, Emily sat.

'You're going to explain?' she asked without much hope, and the laughter was back again.

'I might.' And then the smile died. 'Em, Anna needs me but she won't let me close. Regardless of the outcome of her tests, I need to be here for her for a while. Thank you for getting those tests organised so quickly, by the way,' he added. 'Breast Screen in Blairglen rang an hour ago and said they've fitted Anna in at ten-thirty tomorrow.' He gave a rueful shake of his head. 'Though I'm afraid that means I can't start work properly until the day after tomorrow.'

'You can't start work properly...'

'Em, Anna doesn't let me near,' he said, still with the patience of someone dealing with a person who was terminally stupid. 'Kevin—Anna's de facto husband—was a creep who treated Anna like dirt. I knew he was a creep at the outset. I was unwise enough to say so, and it's haunted me ever since. She kept me away while she was with him, and she probably stayed with him far too long just to prove me wrong. And now she needs me, though she won't admit it. She's desperate for help.'

'She's very proud.'

'Too damned proud,' Jonas growled, and Em gave him a curious look. How would he like it if the shoe were on the other foot? she thought, and she knew instinctively that this man was as independent as his sister.

But he wasn't thinking of his independence now. 'There's a large bridge for us to build, and it isn't going to happen overnight,' he told her, and Em nodded.

'Do you have other family?' she asked curiously, and he shook his head.

'No. There's only Anna and me. That's probably why this has happened. After our Dad died, I was overly protective. She had to rebel and a miserable partnership with an undeserving creep was the result.'

'You can't blame yourself for ever,' she told him, and received another of his blinding smiles for her pains.

'No. I can't. But I can still try and help her. If you'll let me.'

'Like...how?'

'By employing me.'

She looked up at him. He was large and self-possessed and supremely sure of himself, she thought. And she didn't need Dominic's words to know he was competent. She just had to look at him to know that this was a surgeon with skill.

And yet...

'A surgeon wants to work in Bay Beach?' Her voice was incredulous. It sounded unbelievable.

It *was* unbelievable.

'Only for a month or two. Depending...'

'Depending on what?'

'On Anna's diagnosis.'

'You want to be here for her.'

'Of course.' It was simply said, but Em knew she was hearing the truth. And it stunned her. How many high-powered city surgeons would drop their lifestyles for their sister's sake?

'You can take time off?' she asked, and he nodded—as if his decision was of no importance.

'Yes. As it happens, I was about to take an overseas posting—a teaching job in Scotland. I came down here to say goodbye to Anna, and found her in such a state that

I put the job on hold. I knew whatever was frightening
her wasn't going to go away fast, and I need time. To
build those bridges.'

Once again he'd taken her breath away. To simply walk
away from his profession…

'Why not stay with Anna, then?' she suggested. 'I assume you're not married? If you've been on surgeon's
wages, then surely you can just take a holiday.'

'Anna won't let me stay with her, and if there's no good
reason for me to stay in the town then she'll reject me
completely. I'm staying in a hotel—I'm not even staying
with her now. As I said, we have a long way to go.'

He was totally brisk—businesslike in what seemed, to
him, to be a very sensible arrangement. 'Which reminds
me,' he said, ignoring her raised eyebrows. 'If I'm working here as a doctor, are there doctors' quarters where I
can stay?'

'Nowhere big enough for you,' she said without thinking, and his ready laughter sprang back.

'Hey, I'm not *that* big.'

Maybe not in size, but in presence, Em thought a little
desperately, and she tried hard to get her scattered wits in
order. OK. He needed accommodation. He'd help out for
a month or so, but he needed somewhere to stay.

The thought of his help was tantalising. Even if he just
did a couple of nights' call a week he'd be a blessing, she
thought wistfully. Two nights' guaranteed sleep a week…

'I can willingly share your load,' he said softly, and she
blinked. Heck, was she so transparent?

'I can manage on my own.'

'Just like Anna.'

'We don't have a choice,' she snapped, and with that
the laughter died completely.

'Yes,' he told her, and a trace of sternness sounded in

his tone. 'You do have a choice. I'm here for both of you—if you let me.'

Jonas meant it.

He was absolutely positive, he'd brook no argument, and an hour later Em watched him drive away in his exotic little Alfa Romeo while she blinked back her disbelief.

She had a partner—for a month.

'Maybe for more if I need to be here for longer,' he'd growled, and then had added, 'And, please, God, I don't need it.'

She could only agree with him. Please, let Anna not have cancer. But if she did then Em would welcome Jonas with open arms while they waited for Anna to heal, she decided. To share her workload would be bliss. Her surgery was big enough for both of them.

But…her home?

That was the only part of the arrangement which left her less than satisfied. The doctors' house at the back of the hospital had been optimistically built to accommodate up to four doctors. It therefore had four bedrooms and four bathrooms. Em, and her ancient dog, Bernard, rattled around in it.

But it still only had one living room and one kitchen!

So Jonas was heading back to his hotel tonight, but as of tomorrow she'd have him permanently under her feet.

A partner and a housemate—for a month!

But not until tomorrow, she told herself desperately. By then she should have time to get her wayward emotions under control!

Em met Jonas again sooner than the next day. She met him that night.

Two hours later, Em parked outside Home Two, one

of the homes making up Bay Beach Orphanage, and recognised the car parked out front straight away.

How many people in town drove silver Alfa Romeos? None that she knew of, she thought. Except Jonas.

What on earth was *he* doing here?

Drat her stupid emotions, she thought. Why did the sight of his car make her heart jolt?

As her friend opened the front door, Em had to school her expression to hide her surprise, and she had to force her voice to sound normal. It was no mean feat, but somehow she did it.

'Hi, Lori.' She smiled at her friend but gave a sideways, cautious glance at the Alfa. 'Am I intruding?'

'Of course you're not.' Lori pulled the door wide, allowing her to see Jonas sitting at the kitchen table. He looked up at her and smiled, and Em's heart did that lurching thing she was becoming familiar with and didn't understand in the least. 'Jonas and I are having a cup of tea. Do you have time to join us?'

'I might have,' Em said, wary. 'Thanks to Jonas.'

'He told me about taking over your surgery.' Lori pressed her friend's hand. 'And about Charlie. Em, I'm so sorry.'

'It's OK.'

But it wasn't. She'd hardly had time to think of Charlie, but now she blinked back unexpected tears. Damn, she had to give herself time to mourn.

When would she fit that in? Tuesday week, eleven to twelve?

'I... Maybe I won't have that tea. I'll just see Robby and then I'll go,' she told Lori. Robby was the reason she'd come. Whatever Jonas was here for, she had to concentrate on her work.

Which was Robby.

And he needed concentration. Robby was eight months old. He'd been orphaned in a car crash two months ago. Badly burned, he'd only recently been transferred from hospital to the Bay Beach Home.

Robby still really needed city medical facilities—physiotherapy, occupational therapy and the associated bevy of health-care services—but his aunt lived in Bay Beach and she wouldn't hear of him going anywhere else.

Neither would she take him in herself—or allow the thought of someone else adopting him. So Robby was being cared for by Lori at the home, with Em providing daily medical care.

There were worse fates, Em thought. Lori offered no long-term solution for the little boy, but she loved him to bits.

As did Em. Robby had spent two weeks in hospital in Sydney and then, at his aunt's insistence, had spent six weeks at Bay Beach General Hospital. In that time he'd twisted himself around Em's heart like a hairy worm, so much so that when she entered his bedroom now and the little boy reached up his arms, she pulled him to her and hugged as hard as his burned little body would allow.

He was tiny, underweight for his age, with scarring, healing wounds and skin grafts still covering his left side. He'd been burned right up to his chin. The only parts of him that seemed unhurt were his bright little brown eyes, his snub nose and his mop of silver blond curls.

Yes, Em loved him. She'd unashamedly lost her professional detachment, and she'd lost her heart completely.

'Have you been waiting for me?' she whispered. 'I thought you'd be asleep, you ragamuffin!'

'He's supposed to be.' Lori had followed her friend into the room. 'He's been down for half an hour. But he's so accustomed to seeing you in the evenings that I can't get him to sleep until you come.'

'What's the problem?' Em started at the sound of the deep tones. Jonas also had followed them in and was leaning against the door, watching them.

Em and baby were quite a pair, he thought, and if Em could have known what he was thinking she would have blushed to her socks.

She was a strikingly good-looking woman, tall and dark and beautiful, and now, with the child pressed against her breast, she looked stunningly maternal. Robby was still heavily bandaged. He wore a smooth elastic skin to stop his grafts from scarring, and his white dressings were in stark contrast to Em's smooth and darker skin.

The sight set Jonas back more than he cared to admit. He shifted against the door and rephrased his question. 'What happened to the baby?'

And Lori told him, while he watched Em's skilful hands lift away dressings and elastic to check the healing wounds.

He could have helped, he thought—it took several minutes and Lori assisted, but with Jonas's help it would have been quicker—but he was content, for the moment, to watch.

He was getting to know Emily Mainwaring, and the more he saw, the more he approved.

'What?' Em said crossly, as she taped the last dressing, and he started at her tone.

'I beg your pardon?'

'You've been staring at me for ten minutes. I suppose you *have* seen burns dressed before.'

'I have,' He smiled at her, defusing her crossness. 'Many times.'

'There's nothing different here.'

'By the look of those burns, he should still be in hospital,' Jonas said cautiously, feeling his way. Lori was watching both of them with interest, but the tension was all between Jonas and Em.

'Probably. He has more skin grafts to go,' Em told him, once more gathering the little boy to her breast and cradling him like her own. 'But he was becoming institutionalised. I couldn't bear it.'

'And Lori's a good house mother?'

'The best,' Em said warmly, and looked over Robby's fuzzy head at her friend. 'We've had some wonderful housemothers here. Wendy. Erin. The most committed women... And Lori's the absolute best.'

'I'm glad to hear it,' Jonas said simply. 'I suspected as much, and I'm grateful. I persuaded Lori to look after Anna's kids today on a temporary basis—I gather she's the only home mother without a full house—but if there's a major problem and Anna needs an operation then they'll need to come here for a while.'

Em frowned, thinking it through. 'Is that possible, Lori?'

'It is,' Lori told her. 'I've just got off the phone from the powers that be. We can juggle it. Jonas wants something concrete to tell his sister tonight. She needs to know that, no matter what, her kids will be safe.'

'She's having second thoughts,' Jonas told Em. 'About having the tests. She says there's no one to look after the children if she has to have an operation, so why bother having the tests at all?'

'She's badly frightened,' Em said, and he nodded.

'I know. That's why everything has to be settled and easy.'

'You don't think you could assure her you'd take care of the kids yourself?'

'Even if Anna would agree—which she probably wouldn't—I don't think I could,' he admitted honestly, his engaging smile flashing back again. 'They're four, six and eight years old respectively, and I'm a bachelor, born and bred. My childminding skills are about nil. It'd be much easier to work for you and pay Lori to do it.'

'Coward.'

He chuckled out loud. 'Rather be a chicken than a dead hen.' Then he paused. Robby had snuggled into Em's shoulder and was falling asleep before their eyes.

Institutionalised? Maybe not, he thought as he watched. This wasn't a baby who was turning away from the world. The little one was bonding with the adult who'd become permanent. With Em.

And Em knew it. The bonding was a state Em mistrusted, and it was the real reason the little boy was no longer in hospital. She couldn't handle her increasing feelings for him, but she had to keep treating him. Apart from being the only doctor in the place, she couldn't bear not to.

She held him now, and the same familiar longing flooded through her. The longing to hold him for ever had hit unexpectedly when she'd treated him the night his parents had died—the night of the accident—and it had never faded. And, quite simply, she didn't have a clue what to do about it.

'Em, you know Lori and you're great with Anna. I have an idea.' Jonas was speaking to her, and she had to force her attention away from her baby—no, her *patient*—and back to Jonas. He glanced at his watch. 'Have you eaten?'

Eaten? He had to be joking. When did she get dinner before nine at night?

'No,' she said shortly, and he nodded.

'Then can I ask you to eat and then do a house call?'

he said. 'With me? I'll prepay you for the house call with fish and chips on the beach.'

'Fish and chips…'

'You do eat fish and chips?' Once more came his re-signed tone that told her he thought she was a dope, and she had to chuckle. OK, she was acting like one. Maybe she even deserved to be treated as such.

'Sure I eat fish and chips,' she told him. 'You show me a resident of Bay Beach who doesn't! If I'm hungry enough—like now—I'll even eat the newspaper they're wrapped in. But what's your house call?'

'To my sister.'

She'd suspected as much. 'Why?'

'To assure her that Lori is perfectly capable of child-care. She doesn't trust me. It took me three days to have her leave the kids here for two hours this morning. Now I'm working on leaving them here again tomorrow, and then on the possibility of longer-term child care after that. You could help.'

'Why would she listen to me any more than she'd listen to you?'

'She doesn't trust men,' Jonas said simply, and behind them Lori grinned.

'Wise lady.'

'Hey!' Jonas smiled at them both, and spread his hands in mute appeal. 'What's there to mistrust?'

Everything, thought Em, but she didn't say a word.

'Do you have any more urgent calls?' he asked.

'I have an evening ward round.'

'That can wait. I'd imagine you wear a beeper.'

'Of course I wear a beeper.'

'Then I'll help you with your ward round and then the evening's ours,' he told her grandly. 'Apart from house calls and emergencies. What more could two people want?'

What, indeed?

They ate their dinner on the beach because, quite simply, it was the most beautiful and most lonely place to be and what Em needed most was solitude to absorb the fact of Charlie's death.

Strangely, she didn't mind that her much-needed solitude was shared with Jonas, and it didn't seem less peaceful because he was with her. He bought them fish and chips and soda water—'I'd prefer wine but with your workload I'm guessing you'd refuse'—and then settled beside her. Then he let her alone with her thoughts.

Like Em, he seemed content to munch his fish and chips, and stare out to where the moon was just starting to glimmer over the horizon. Somehow, though, he seemed to gaze inward just the same.

So she was left with her thoughts. It was the most beautiful place, Em thought. Charlie had loved this beach.

And Charlie's death was suddenly very, very real.

'You loved him very much,' Jonas said after a while, and Em looked down as his hand moved across to gently cover hers. It wasn't an attempt at intimacy, though. It was a gesture of comfort—nothing more—and it warmed her more than she could say.

There was nothing between them but the truth. 'Yes,' she agreed simply. 'Since Grandpa died we've been even closer. Charlie's always been my best friend, and after Grandpa died he was all I've had.'

'When did your parents die?'

'When I was tiny. They died like Robby's parents. In a car crash.'

'And that's why you feel so strongly about Robby?'

The idea startled her. She hadn't seen it like that but now, looking at it dispassionately, she realised maybe he was right.

'I guess so.'

'Except he doesn't have a Grandpa and a Charlie to love him.'

'Maybe I was lucky.'

'So it seems.' Jonas stirred and poured himself out more soda water. 'I wish I'd known them.'

And suddenly she wished that he'd known them, too. Her two lovely old men.

'They were amazing,' she told him. Her tired grey eyes creased into a smile of memory. 'They were a machiavellian pair of old devils, they got into every mischief they possibly could, but they brought me up so well.'

'I can see that.'

It was a compliment, direct and to the point, and its simplicity made Em flush. 'I didn't mean…'

'I know you didn't,' he said softly. 'If you had, I wouldn't have said it.'

She looked down at him for a long, long moment. He was lying full length on the sand as he sipped his soda water. His hand was still on hers and his big body seemed to go on for ever. He was lazily watching the moon as it slid silently up over the horizon—a thing worth watching—but, by watching it and not her, he made her feel apart from him. As if she still had her solitude yet she wasn't alone.

It was an impossible feeling to describe. Apart, and yet not. Warmed? Warmer than she'd felt for years.

Just…not so alone.

This man was only here for a month, she told herself, shaken more than she cared to admit by the feelings she was experiencing. She was here for life, and he was here for such a short time. And then she'd be alone again...

'Why did you come to practise in Bay Beach?' he asked, and she started. It was as if he'd read her thoughts.

'There was never a choice.'

'Because Grandpa and Charlie were here?'

'That, and the fact that I love Bay Beach.'

'I can't imagine there's much of a social life in Bay Beach?' His statement was a question.

'No, but that's easy.' She grinned. 'As sole doctor, I don't have time for a social life.'

'You do now,' he told her easily. 'While I'm here you can have some free time.'

'Maybe I need to pick up a boyfriend, then,' she said, trying to keep it light. 'For a month. It seems a bit hard on the bloke, though. After a month I go back to being general medico and dogsbody and he'd get what was left over. Which wouldn't be very much at all.'

And then, at the end of her sentence, the lightness faded and she couldn't quite keep the bitterness out of her voice. Jonas heard it as she knew he must.

'You resent it?'

'No.' She shook her head, and her braid swung with decision. 'I don't. At least, I normally don't. It's only sometimes...'

'Like today?'

'Like today,' she agreed. 'I told Claire Fraine to go to Blairglen two weeks before her baby was due. She refused—she said it was stupid as her babies always take ages to come and there'd be plenty of time to get to Blairglen after she went into labour. So what happens? I get to deliver twins in the middle of the night.' She bit her lip.

'And I almost lost one,' she admitted. 'One of the twins

wasn't picked up by Blairglen's obstetrician—heaven knows why—so we were expecting a single baby, and Thomas came by surprise after his much bigger sister. At only three pounds it was pure chance and the prompt arrival of the flying neonatal service that stopped him dying on me.'

'No wonder you're exhausted.'

'Yes, and they don't see,' she said bitterly, 'that by taking chances themselves, they put me at risk.' She shook her head. 'No. That came out wrong. I'm not suggesting I was at risk.'

'But you *were* at risk—at risk of breaking your heart over a needlessly dead baby,' Jonas told her, understanding absolutely. He rose and looked down at her for a long moment, then held out his hands to hers. It was an imperious gesture—he was a man accustomed to getting his own way—and, rather to her own surprise, Em took them. As he gripped her and tugged her to her feet, the feeling of strength communicated itself to her, and it felt strange and warm.

And…dangerous?

But he didn't seem to feel it. 'I've come to a decision. What you need, Dr Mainwaring,' he told her with all due solemnity, 'is a paddle in the surf. And I'm just the person to give it to you. Take your sandals off.'

'Yes, sir.' She was bemused but game.

'And I'll take my shoes and socks off.' He grinned and bent down to do just that. 'Mind, this is no small concession. It's not every woman I'd take my shoes and socks off for.'

'You know, I guessed that?'

He looked up at her and his smile widened.

'Of course you did,' he told her. 'We're partners, after all. And a woman needs to know a lot about her partner. Even if it is only a partnership for a month.'

CHAPTER THREE

THE paddle was a long one—strolling about half a mile away from the town, walking through the small breakers at the edge of the surf. Magically, Em's beeper stayed silent. It was as if the town had thrown its worst at her over the past twenty-four hours, and knew its doctor was close to breaking point. She needed this break more desperately than she even guessed herself.

The moon was completely up now. They should go home. Em should go to bed.

'But Anna never has the children in bed until nine,' Jonas told her. 'It's no use turning up there to talk to her before that. She simply won't listen. And paddling does the soul just as much good as sleeping.'

So they walked. Rather to Em's regret, her hand was released, and they walked side by side, as two friends might have.

Two good friends.

It had to be good friends, she thought, because their silences weren't uneasy. They fell into step and splashed through the shallows in unison, and the sensation was like a balm to Em's troubled mind. She could feel the tension easing out of her, disappearing into the coolness of the surf and washing out to sea.

This was...special.

Em didn't speak, but she soaked it all in—the night, the lovely feel of surf between her toes and the moonlight. And somewhere in that walk her feeling of desperation, of absolute weariness and of isolation, all fell away, and she knew that tonight, babies and emergencies permitting, she'd sleep like a child.

Jonas had granted this to her, she thought, and for that she was incredibly grateful. She still wasn't sure how it had happened, but when the headland met the sea in a rocky outcrop and paddling became impossible, she turned to him impulsively.

'Thank you,' she said.

'For what? For taking a beautiful woman for a walk along the beach?' He smiled down at her. 'It's been my absolute pleasure.'

A beautiful woman...

How long since anyone had called her that? Em thought. Grandpa had, and so had Charlie, but they'd called her beautiful since she was three years old. Back at medical school she'd had a couple of boyfriends, but since moving to Bay Beach... There simply hadn't been time for boyfriends.

No time to be called beautiful?

She grinned wryly at the thought. I should stick that in my diary, she decided, because the thought, silly though it was, was still delicious. Allow time to be described as beautiful.

'What's funny?'

Em smiled up at him, and then resolutely turned her face back along the beach to where Jonas had parked his car. He was driving her tonight, and that in itself was novel. 'Nothing. It's time for us to go and see Anna.'

He fell into step beside her. His trousers were wet to the knees—he'd rolled them up but they'd been splashed anyway and it was too warm a night to care about a spot of wetness, and the surf felt great. Em's dress was soaked almost to the thighs but, like Jonas, she didn't care. She was feeling so light-headed she could almost float.

It was weariness, she told herself. Or reaction to Charlie's death. Or…something!

'You won't tell me the joke?' he demanded.

'Nope.'

'Why not?'

'It's none of your business.'

'Ah, but that's where you're wrong,' he said, and before she knew what he was about his hand caught hers again and swung. 'Because I just succeeded, and I want to know how to do it again.'

'Succeeded?'

'In making you smile.' He twinkled down at her. 'When I first saw you, I thought, I bet that woman has the most magical smile—and she has. Now there's only one thing more I want to know.'

It was impossible not to ask the obvious. 'Which is what?'

'What your hair looks like unbraided,' he threw back at her, and she gasped and lifted her spare hand defensively to the hair in question.

'You'll wait a while for that.'

'Why?' Jonas sounded curious—nothing more. Still his hand held hers and it felt good. It felt…right.

'Because, apart from when I wash it, my hair's unbraided for about five minutes a day,' she said with asperity. 'I rebraid it every night before I go to bed, so it's ready for emergencies.'

'You mean…' he said slowly, looking at her out of the corner of his eye with a look she didn't quite understand. Or didn't quite trust. 'You mean, if I was on call for you, so you wouldn't be at risk of an emergency call, then you'd sleep with your hair unbraided?'

This was a ridiculous question. But he was waiting for an answer. Em kicked up a spray of water before her—

for heaven's sake, she was acting as young and as carefree as a schoolgirl on her first date—and she tilted her chin and told him.

'I might.'

'But it's not definite.' He sounded so disappointed that she almost chuckled out loud.

'I probably would,' she said, just to placate him. Or just to make him smile.

And she succeeded. 'That'd make me feel so much better,' he told her. 'If I get called out to someone's ingrown toenail, and I'm whittling away at rotten nail at three in the morning and smelling some farmer's stinking feet, it'd make me feel a whole heap better knowing that my partner was sleeping at home with her hair splayed out all over the pillow…'

'And with her dog beside her and her door firmly locked!' She said it as a reaction, like she was slamming her hand on the lock right now!

'Really?' He sounded shocked at the thought of such distrust, and Em could contain herself no longer. Her laughter rang out over the waves. This man was ridiculous. Deliciously ridiculous, but ridiculous all the same.

'Yes, Dr Lunn, with my door locked,' she told him. 'Do you think I'm naïve or something?'

In answer, the hold on her hand tightened even further.

'You wouldn't have to lock the door,' he said virtuously. 'Because I'd be out chopping up toenails.' And then his voice flattened. 'And, no, Dr Mainwaring,' he told her, and his voice was suddenly deadly serious, 'I think you're all sorts of things. But I definitely don't think you're naïve.'

He'd caught her right off her guard. She wasn't ready for seriousness. 'Jonas…'

'Emily…' He matched her tone of uncertainty exactly, and it was all she could do not to laugh again.

'You're impossible! Jonas, we need to see Anna.'

'So we do.' He sighed. 'So we do. But we can come back here another night. No?'

'Maybe.'

'What sort of answer is that?' Once more his voice had changed and now he sounded indignant. It was impossible not to laugh.

'It's a safe answer,' she told him, and then because suddenly she didn't feel safe in the least—she felt very, very exposed—she hauled her hand from his and started to run. 'I'll beat you to the car, Jonas Lunn,' she called.

She ran.

Rather to her surprise, Jonas didn't follow suit. Instead, he stopped dead, and watched her flying figure in the moonlight, racing up the sandhills toward his waiting car.

And his smile slowly died.

'I wonder if I'm being really, really stupid here,' he asked himself—but there was nothing but the moon and the surf to answer him.

Jonas had been right.

Anna was terrified and ready to back out, and it took his and Em's combined persuasion to keep her on track.

'We've made the appointment.' Jonas went through it slowly and surely. 'And we've organised everything else that needs to be done. You drop Sam and Matt at school and take Ruby to Lori's, and then I take you to Blairglen for the tests. If we're delayed—if you need more tests than a mammogram and biopsy—then Lori will collect the children and give them their dinner.'

'But they'll put me straight into hospital. If it's cancer—'

'They won't,' Em said strongly, and put her hand out to cover Anna's. The woman was trembling. This fear was the culmination of a month's imaginings, Em thought. How much better it would have been if she'd just confronted the thing head-on when she'd first found the lump, rather than wait until it had built into this icy terror.

'Anna, a few days now will make no difference to the outcome at all,' she told her decisively. 'No matter what the results of the tests are, there's time to come home and think about it. Savour the feeling that it's just a cyst. Or come to terms with the fact that you have an early breast cancer before you need surgery. Either way, no one's going to rush you into something you're unhappy with.'

Anna looked desperately from her brother to Em and back again.

'But Jonas has already spoken to Lori about taking the kids long-term.'

'That's just so, if the worst comes to the worst, you know you can face it,' Em told her, and received a grateful glance from Jonas for her pains. 'Prepare for the worst and hope for the best. It's my personal creed and I remember it every time my phone rings.'

There was a pause while Anna thought that through. Then...

'That must be terrible,' Anna said slowly, for the first time looking at Em and really seeing her. 'I hadn't thought about it before, but now... It's the not knowing that's the worst, and in your job all the time there'll be not knowing. Like that awful tractor accident last week. You had to deal with that, didn't you?'

'It *was* dreadful,' Em said gently. 'At the time it was frightening. But once I knew what I was dealing with, the fear faded as I worked through what had to be done.

That's exactly the same as you. Tomorrow you'll know what you're dealing with.'

'I don't know how you do it,' Anna whispered, and that was the cue for Jonas to take her other hand.

'Anna…'

To Em's surprise she pulled away from her brother. 'Don't!'

'I just wanted to say that I'm here for you. I'll take you for the test tomorrow, but I'm staying on in Bay Beach.'

His words obviously shocked her. 'Why?'

'For you,' he said promptly, but Anna shook her head at that.

'No way, Jonas. I don't need you.' She bit her lip and stared at the table. 'I've never needed you—just like I never needed Dad and I never needed Kevin. You're not to stay on my account.'

What was behind this? Anna thought, puzzled. There was more history here than a brother antagonistic toward a sister's partner.

But Jonas was shaking his head, and smiling at his sister as if he was reassuring her that he really didn't want to intrude—that things were as she wanted them.

'I'm not staying because of you—Stoopid,' he told her.

'I wish you'd stop calling me that silly name.' Unconsciously Anna's hand clenched so that the whites of her knuckles showed through her skin. She was too thin, Em thought. Too young and too tired and too battered by life.

'OK.' Jonas's smile died. He stood and, surprisingly, he moved to stand behind Emily. His hands dropped down to grip her shoulders but he still spoke to his sister. 'I won't call you Stoopid any more.'

'Fine. And you don't have to stay.'

'I do have to stay,' he said gently. 'Because Em needs me.'

'Em?'

'I couldn't believe what Em was facing this morning,' he told his sister, with his big hands still resting lightly on Emily's shoulders. 'You saw yourself what a strain she was under, and it knocked me sideways. I know I'm due to leave for overseas, but I've decided to put it off. I'm staying put.'

'With…with Dr Mainwaring.'

'With Emily,' he corrected her. 'With one of the most hard-working, beautiful, desirable lady doctors I've ever had the pleasure to meet. Em and I have it all worked out.'

'I don't believe this.'

Neither did Em. Heavens, the way he talked—the way he was holding her—the man sounded as if he was in love with her!

And he did exactly nothing to change that impression.

'Em and I have spent the last two hours on the beach,' he told Anna. 'We've been working things out. It may be sudden, but it doesn't mean it hasn't happened.' The grip on Em's shoulders tightened—either in affection or as a warning. Even afterwards, Em couldn't quite figure out which.

'I'm not leaving Emily,' he told his sister. 'We're partners.'

'I—'

'So I'm here for you as well,' he told her, his voice brooking no argument. 'But mostly I'm here for Em. And I'm here for as long as she wants me. Whether you want me or not.'

'Jonas—'

'Leave it, Anna,' he told her roughly. 'For now let's

just get these damned tests done. But I'm staying in the town—with Emily—for as long as it takes. And maybe even longer.'

'You're nuts!' Back in the car, Em looked at the man beside her as if she were regarding a lunatic. 'You've implied it was love at first sight between us.'

'I did it beautifully,' he said smugly, and she could have slapped him.

'You did it intentionally?'

'Sure.'

She sat back and gazed straight ahead. Doctor encountering lunatic and wondering where the nearest straitjacket was. How was she supposed to react to this?

'Um...do you have a reason?' she asked finally, and her voice came out sort of as a surprised squeak. It didn't sound in the least like a doctor soothing a lunatic. He heard it and he grinned.

'There's no need to take this personally.'

'Oh, sure.' Still the squeak. Em coughed and got her voice back under control—almost. 'Sure. You imply to your sister that you're in love with me and I'm not supposed to take it personally.'

'Do you have any more work to do tonight?'

'Stop changing the subject.'

'No, but do you?' Jonas was gently insistent. 'Because if you have any more calls, I can take you there before I drop you back at the hospital.'

'So you can fit in a spot of love-making on the side,' she said nastily, and the twerp actually laughed.

'Hey, there's an idea.'

'A very bad idea.' She glowered.

'You don't approve of love-making?'

'With men I like and trust,' she retorted, and he winced at that.

'Ouch.'

'So there you go. Take me home.'

'You do know I have my reasons,' he said slowly, and she was forced to nod.

'I guess I do. You can't be totally unhinged or they'd never had given you your medical degree.'

'There is that.' His smile faded and he looked at the road ahead. 'Em, you know Anna won't let me close. I've battled every inch of the way to get her this far, and it's only because she's terrified that she let me come with her this morning. She was ready to clutch anyone. Once Anna has her head sorted again, I'll be thrust back on the sidelines. She doesn't want me.'

'I'd assume she has her reasons.'

'Maybe.'

Silence. The laughter had faded completely, and for once Jonas had his face set in grim lines. He wouldn't tell her unless she asked, Em thought, but, then, she was a family doctor. She was accustomed to asking hard questions.

'And the reasons would be…'

'Do you really want to know?'

'I want to know everything about my lover's family,' she said primly, and got a wry smile for her pains.

'Touché.'

'So tell me.'

More silence. Anna's house was on the far side of the headland to the hospital—about ten minutes' drive. They were driving along the coast road. The moon was glinting off the sea, and the sound of the surf was thrumming into the open windows of Jonas's lovely car. It was a night for lovers, Em thought inconsequentially. And Jonas had declared he was one.

But it was a lie. It had been said for a purpose—to achieve something. And that something was *nothing* to do with Emily.

'My father was an alcoholic,' he said at last, and Em frowned into the night.

'Tough?'

'Very tough.' There was grit in his words, and a lifetime of pain behind them. 'Our mother couldn't take it. She wasn't what you call a strong character. When I was twelve and Anna was nine, she met someone else and simply walked away. Leaving us with Dad.'

There was silence while Em thought this one through. She knew what an alcoholic parent meant—she had a couple of troubled kids in her practice for just that reason— and she didn't like what she was thinking.

'You want to tell me about it?' she said at last, and he nodded.

'Not much, but maybe I need to if you agree to play onside.'

'You mean, pretend to be your lover.'

'Pretend to need me.' Once more that quick, inconsequential grin and Em's insides did that funny lurch again. She *loved* this man's smile. 'Not that you don't, of course.'

'Of course,' she said primly. 'But just medically.'

'And not in your bed.'

'I have an ancient mutt called Bernard,' she told him, making her mouth stern. 'I rescued him from the pound when he was about a hundred which makes him about a hundred and ten now. He acts as my bedwarmer, and he's all I need.'

'Lucky old Bernard. Has *he* seen you with your hair down?'

'Dr Lunn, are you going to tell me what the problem is with Anna, or are you going to let me out of the car?' Em snapped. 'I'm getting fed up here.'

'Whereas I'm enjoying myself. And I don't much want to talk about my father.'

'But you need to tell me.' She was a doctor, after all, and pressing a point home was what she was good at. It had to be if she was to survive a morning's surgery without being swamped by inconsequential gossip.

'There's nothing much to tell.' Once more the laughter faded, and Jonas concentrated on the road ahead. 'My father was charming, handsome, kind, witty…'

Just like his son, Em thought, but didn't say so.

'And he was also an irretrievable drunk. He could charm anything out of anybody. Anna loved him so much that even if our mother had wanted us to go with her— which she didn't—I don't think Anna would have gone. She believed in him, you see. He lied to her over and over, and every time he let her down she made excuses for him. After our mother left, most of those excuses centred around me.'

'I don't understand.'

'He lied all the time,' Jonas said bleakly. 'Until recently—just before he died when he told me so much I didn't know—I wasn't aware how badly. But he'd promise Anna a party dress and then say I'd spent all his money that week. Or he'd swear he'd take her out for her fifteenth birthday and then tell her he had to be away because I was in trouble at university. I was paying my way through uni, taking every job I could, but Dad never told Anna that. Sure, she knew I worked, but Dad always implied all his spare money went to me. So there was nothing for her. Ever.'

'Oh, Jonas…'

'There was worse,' Jonas said grimly. 'But you don't want to know. Enough to say that I was always the evil one. Dad treated me like that all the time. He blamed me for my mother going. It got worse when I applied to stop his pension and funnel it through social welfare. That meant Anna had at least enough to eat. And even as a student, some of the money I worked for went to him. But he hated it. He hated that I was in any sort of control.'

'But someone had to be.'

'As you say.'

She took this on board, thinking of another child she knew with an alcoholic father—one of her patients, and a child so much older than his years that she ached for him. 'And then…' she prodded gently.

'And then Anna met Kevin—who was just like Dad.' Once more, Jonas's voice was filled with bitterness. 'Kevin was handsome and he made her laugh and he drank like a fish. And he depended on her. Like Dad.'

He shrugged slowly into the dark. 'Anna and I…we've been taught the hard way not to depend on people, but we don't mind people depending on us. Like our parents. So she fell blindly in love, or she thought she did, and when I tried to intervene she hated me for it. And the more right I was, the more she hated me.'

'That must have been hell!'

'It was,' he said bitterly. And then added, 'It still is.'

'She still holds it against you?'

'I guess.' He shrugged. 'But I love my little sister, Em, and I'm doing everything I can to get her life back on track. Now Kevin's gone I have a chance. Unless this bloody disease…'

'Hey!' Unconsciously Em's hand flew across to rest on his on the steering-wheel. 'Hey, Jonas, you know the odds. They're very, very good.'

'Yeah, but it's a scary word—cancer,' he told her, and she pressed his hand once more.

'Try cyst, then,' she said softly. 'Until tomorrow.'

'You don't think it's a cyst. It'll be cancer and maybe it'll have spread. Good things don't happen to our family.' His hands clenched and clenched again and again on the steering-wheel, and she could feel the strain in the muscles under her hand. 'Good things don't happen to Anna.'

'I think they do,' she said softly.

He gave a harsh laugh. 'And how do you figure that one out?'

'Because she has you,' she said gently. 'Because you're with her every step of the way.'

'She won't let me be.'

'As my partner, you can't be anywhere else,' she told him.

'You agree—to play along?'

'I agree that I need you,' she said simply. 'For as long as it takes.'

And that was that.

Only it wasn't quite as simple as he had made out, Em thought as she lay waiting for sleep that night. Blessedly the hospital was quiet. Last night's twins had been airlifted to Sydney, Henry Tozer's gallstones, which had troubled both Henry and Em last night, had finally settled and peace reigned over the wards.

Bernard was snoring peacefully at the foot of the bed. All was right with his world.

Em should have done the same. Instead, she lay and

stared into the darkness and wondered about the promise she'd just made.

If indeed Anna's lump turned out to be malignant, then Jonas might well want to stay for her operation and afterwards, for the further weeks of radiotherapy and possibly chemo. Em figured it out in her head. It'd take at least three months, she thought. She could have him here for three months.

And all the time he'd be pretending he was staying for Em's sake, and not Anna's.

That was all very well, she thought, but where did that leave her?

Bernard stirred and whoofled in his sleep—which amounted to the ancient mutt's complete exercise for the day. Em hauled him close and hugged his portly frame, but he was already asleep again. She arranged him back at her feet, like some huge, hairy pyjama-bag, then lay back and fingered her firmly braided hair.

She was close to thirty, she told herself, and here she was, sleeping in a single bed with a dog who stayed awake all of sixty seconds per day! And that was to eat. All of a sudden she had an almost irresistible urge to unbraid her hair and shift the snoring Bernard out of the room.

'But I won't do it,' she told the battered old dog, and she knew she wouldn't. 'You're my constant, Bernard Heinz. Bay Beach needs a dedicated doctor, and I'm it. Now Charlie's gone, you're the only male in my life, and that's the way it's going to stay. Now and for ever.'

For ever...

CHAPTER FOUR

EMILY made the journey to Blairglen the following morning, specifically to see Anna at the end of her tests. She knew Jonas was with her but, if she could, she needed to be there, too.

Luckily, it was Tuesday. Em had an arrangement with a doctor who worked south of Bay Beach. They were both overworked, but in emergencies they gave anaesthetics for each other, or covered if one was ill. They'd formalised this so that every Tuesday Chris was officially 'on call' for Em, and every Thursday she did the same for him.

It didn't give them time off. What it meant was that they could do house calls in outlying areas where the cellphones were out of range, and while they did it they knew the nursing staff had someone they could contact in an emergency.

And this Tuesday it meant that Em could rise early, check her hospital patients, visit a patient on the northernmost tip of her district and then travel the extra distance to end up at Blairglen Hospital.

Blairglen Breast Screen in particular.

Anna's mammogram had been scheduled for ten-thirty so Anna was well through the X-ray department by the time she got there. As referring doctor, Em asked to see the X-rays before she saw Anna, and her heart sank at what was put up on the screen.

This didn't look like a cyst.

On the other hand, she told herself firmly, deliberately thinking positively, it looked a firmly contained mass.

There was only the one small lump, and there was no other suspicious area.

'Where's Anna now?' she asked the nurse in charge, and was pointed through into the procedures room.

'They've done an ultrasound, and now they're doing a biopsy,' the nurse told her. 'But she's seen the X-rays and her brother's explained what it means. He's nice, isn't he? He's still with her.'

Yes, he was nice, but Em was focused on Anna. 'Can I go in?'

'Sure,' the nurse told her.

So Em went in. Anna was lying on the procedure trolley, while a biopsy was taken. The medical team were taking tiny core samples of the tumour.

They weren't wasting any time, Anna thought. Which was good. By the end of today they'd have solid answers. That was something, at least, even if the answers weren't the ones they'd hoped for.

From the door, Em could hardly see Anna, but she saw Jonas at once. He looked up as she entered, and she saw straight away the strain and shock he was feeling.

It was impossible to be doctor and brother at the same time, she thought, and her heart went out to him. What had the nurse said? He'd explained the X-rays to Anna? Surely that wasn't his job.

But her focus now still had to be on Anna. She crossed to the table, a nurse made room for her and she lifted Anna's hand as the doctors worked on.

'Hi,' she told her. 'Not great news, huh?'

Anna shook her head, and a tear slipped down her cheek. She looked terrible, clothed in a pallid, green hospital gown, her face bloodless, and only her bright hair giving any vestige of colour. The doctor was taking a biopsy of her breast at that moment. Even though she was anaesthetised and there'd be no pain, Anna's lips were clenched, and Em saw she was very close to the edge.

Without a word Em grabbed a tissue, held it to Anna's eyes, and then placed it in her hand. 'The specimen's been taken,' she told her as the doctor moved away. 'Anna, it's finished. That's the last of the tests.'

'It's cancer.'

'Yes, it's cancer. Anna, this is bad news, but not terrible. You hang on to that.' She flicked a glance at the radiologist in charge, a woman in her fifties. 'This probably won't even mean a mastectomy, will it, Margaret?'

'Not on the basis of what we've found.' Margaret White was Blairglen's senior radiologist. Normally, to do a mastectomy or not was a surgeon's decision, but Patrick May, who did Blairglen's breast surgery, worked hand in glove with Margaret and he didn't mind if Margaret stepped in with early reassurance. 'You'll be using Patrick?'

'That's who I'll be suggesting,' Em said. She took Anna's hand and smiled down at her. 'Anna, Patrick May is one of the best surgeons I've met.' She hesitated and then smiled again. 'Apart from your brother, of course.'

That brought a weak twinkle in response, as Anna looked up at Jonas's strained face. 'Of...of course.'

'Patrick's good,' Em reiterated, for the benefit of Jonas, who was looking doubtful. 'If you—and Jonas—are happy to use him and you have the operation here, we can transfer you back to Bay Beach Hospital for aftercare almost immediately. That means the kids can visit you.

'But the chemotherapy...radiotherapy...how will I cope?'

'Radiotherapy is just like having a chest X-ray once a day. And if the tumor's as tiny and self-contained as it looks, then chemotherapy would be optional extra insurance. That's all. Do it and get on with your life.' Anna closed her eyes. 'You're not lying to me?' she asked weakly. 'You're not all lying?'

Em's hand tightened on hers. 'Absolutely not.'

'How the hell did you manage it?'

Anna was dressing, and Jonas had hauled Em out into the corridor, out of Anna's hearing. 'How did you get away from Bay Beach to be here for Anna?' His voice was incredulous, as if he was having trouble taking everything in. 'You could have floored me when you walked through the door.'

'Miracles sometimes happen,' Em said lightly, and glanced at her watch. 'I work on producing them when they're needed. But...' She hesitated. 'This miracle is due to end. I can't be here for long.'

'For long enough. You were the person she most wanted to see.'

'I figured that,' Em said seriously, accepting it as the truth. 'Half the fear of this type of investigation is that it has to be done by strangers. So, when I can, I try to get here.'

'You'd do this for anybody?'

She stiffened. 'You mean, I'd do it not just for your sister?'

He gave a weary smile at that, and an apologetic shrug. 'I guess you must. Anna is special to me, but to you she's just a patient.'

'No one's just a patient,' Em said roundly. 'And if I ever feel like that, I'll walk away from medicine and never come back.'

There was a sudden silence. A nurse walked by, carrying a tray of pathology specimens, but she was ignored. Jonas was watching Em, and he had eyes for nobody else.

'City GPs don't do this for their patients,' Jonas said slowly, and Em shook her head.

'That's unfair. How many family doctors do you know?'

'It's not unfair. It's true.'

'Then your knowledge of family medicine is biased,' she told him. She smiled then, determined to keep things light. 'What a good thing you're going to be one for a couple of months.'

'A couple of months...'

'Three,' she said promptly. 'That's how long at least Anna will need you.'

'If she lets me.'

'She'll let you. So you're facing three months of trying to be a good brother and a good family doctor. It's going to be quite a learning experience.' She shook her head and glanced at her watch. 'Jonas, I really need to go.'

'I know.'

But she didn't want to leave.

And Jonas himself didn't want her to go. She could feel it. There was a moment's silence while Em looked at the floor and Jonas looked at Em. Wondering.

And then, before she could stop him, he reached out and took her hands in his. Both her hands. He held them tightly, looking down at them with a twisted, self-mocking smile.

They were good hands, he could see. Em's hands bore the scars of too much use—of being washed a hundred times a day, every day of the week, for years and for years as she moved from patient to patient. These weren't the hands of the women he normally mixed with, he thought, but they looked wonderful hands to him.

'Thank you, Emily,' he said simply, and then he did the only thing he could think of to do—and he did it because he couldn't bear not to.

Right there and then, in the busy hospital corridor, with people striding by every few seconds, he pulled her into his arms and he kissed her.

And by the time he'd let her go, Em's life had changed for ever.

'I do not care for Jonas Lunn!'

Em said it to herself over and over, like a mantra, as she drove back to Bay Beach, and all afternoon and evening she worked with the same mantra ringing in her head. He's a charismatic bachelor who's drop-dead gorgeous. He kissed you out of gratitude, and it means absolutely nothing at all. And even if it did mean anything…even if he's attracted to you like you are to him…he's here for a short time while his sister is treated and then he's off. He's out of here, and you have to carry on with your life!

But it wasn't quite as simple as that. The mantra had flaws. Because…

Because—'He's gorgeous!' Lori said, as Em dropped by to treat her little burns patient that night. She was watching as Em changed dressings and made Robby's small limbs do their exercises, but Lori's mind wasn't on Robby. It was definitely on Jonas. 'He's one of the best-looking men I've seen.'

And then she watched with interest as her friend's colour turned to a slow-burn crimson. Her eyebrows rose. 'Hey, and you think so, too.'

'But, then, I'm sex-starved,' Em retorted, and she managed a grin. She was trying desperately to keep it light. 'Me and my old Bernard have a thing going, but I'll admit the relationship's been rocky lately. Bernard's snoring's getting out of hand and, frankly, Jonas Lunn doesn't look bad in comparison.'

'In comparison to a moth-eaten mongrel who does nothing but sleep and whose only party trick is to trip people over when they least expect it? Wow, that's saying something.' Lori watched as Em's deft fingers gently massaged Robby's legs. 'Robby's doing really well.'

'He is.' Em smiled down at baby Robby, who smiled just as happily up at her. Even when she hurt him he smiled at her, she thought, and her heart twisted again. Damn. Robby and now Jonas were twisting their way into her heart. Bernard was facing some pretty stiff competition these days.

'Robby'll have two brothers and a sister as of tomorrow,' Lori told her, and watched her face change.

'You mean Anna's kids are coming here while she has the operation?'

'Yep. Anna and Jonas were here two hours back, collecting the kids but organising a longer-term stay for them. Apparently the surgeon wants to operate as soon as possible and, now she's made up her mind, Anna can't see any reason for putting it off. So it's tomorrow. In fact, I think she would have liked to get it over with this afternoon.'

'I don't blame her.' Em nodded as she thought it through. 'So Jonas is dumping the kids on you.'

'That's hardly fair,' Lori said mildly. 'He'll be back and forth, visiting Anna, he's offered to work for you—which I think is a really good idea—and he's hopeless with kids. He hardly knows them.' She shrugged. 'And we're lucky. For once, the homes aren't full. Kate and Anna—the twins who've been with me while their parents sorted themselves out—left me yesterday, no one's been sent down from Sydney and Robby is all I have left.'

Then, as Em finished Robby's dressing, Lori scooped the baby up and hugged him tight. 'That leaves just me and Robby tonight, doesn't it, scamp?'

But not quite. Robby pursed his lips and his little mouth puckered. He held himself rigid against Lori, twisted his tiny body and held out his arms to Em. It was absolutely transparent where his affections lay.

Damn.

Lori handed him over, but her pucker of concern remained. 'He's still attached to you, Em.'

'Maybe it'd be best if I didn't see him any more,' Em said, but her heart flinched at the thought. She had to harden it. Long-term commitment to a baby wasn't an option. 'Now Jonas will be here every day—at least I assume he'll be here, checking on his niece and nephews—he could do the dressing changes.'

'Which leaves Robby with no one.'

'It leaves him with you. He has to reattach some time, and it mustn't be to me.'

'I don't know to who, then,' Lori said. 'It's a disaster if he attaches long-term to me. I'm just an interim home mother. I must get his aunt to agree to long-term foster care.'

'She still won't?'

'No. She has the attitude that the town will think she's uncaring—that it's a betrayal of her sister to put Robby into foster-care.'

'So she'll leave him in an orphanage instead!'

'When in doubt, do nothing,' Lori said, and there was a trace of weariness in her voice which Em caught.

'Maybe we could have Jonas talk to her,' she suggested. 'He can charm blood out of a stone, that one.'

'He can at that.' Lori looked at her friend, and her attention focused. 'Are you sure you're not interested in him?'

'I'm not interested in him.'

'You know...' Lori looked her up and down, noting how tightly her hands were holding the little boy in her arms, and noting also the signs of strain around her eyes. 'You know, I don't believe you.'

'You'd better.' Em glowered. 'If you find Jonas so attractive, why don't you have an affair with him yourself?'

'Oh, great.' Lori grinned placidly. 'No, thanks. I have my Raymond, and he's a far sexier being than even your Bernard!'

That brought a chuckle. 'I don't know about that,' Em said innocently, thinking of Lori's boyfriend, Bay Beach's local accountant, with a grin. 'They look about the same around the middle. And with the weight Ray's carrying, I bet they snore the same.'

She got a glower back—and then a chuckle of agreement. 'OK, you're right,' Lori said fondly. 'Poor Raymond. But he has taken on board what you said about the dangers to his heart. He's been on a diet for weeks now.'

'That's great,' Em said, mildly surprised. Lori's Raymond was verging on truly fat, and she worried about him, but she thought he'd taken on the role of fat and jovial for ever.

'It's not much use, though,' Lori told her, still smiling. 'It's just lucky I love him tubby. He's using the doughnut hole diet.'

'The doughnut hole diet?'

'Doughnut holes are the bits you get when you cut the middle out of the doughnut.' Lori nodded sagely. 'So, instead of eating donuts, Ray now only eats doughnut holes. He figures all the calories stay in the doughnuts themselves.' She chuckled. 'And yet still I love him. If I wasn't so tied up with my kids I'd even marry him—but he's content enough with the arrangement as it is.'

'Lucky Ray.'

'Lucky me.' Her friend's smile died. 'Seriously, Em, you'll be sharing a house with Jonas for the next three months. If I were you—'

'If I were me I'd be very careful,' Em said solidly. 'Unlike you, I can't indulge in a love life. Seriously, Lori, do you know what would happen if I fell in love with Jonas Lunn?'

'No.' Her friend sighed resignedly. 'I don't. But I have a feeling you're about to tell me.'

'Yep.' Em was on her bandwagon now, and there was no stopping her. 'It's one of two things. First, I could fall completely irrevocably in love, my passion would be returned in full by the wonderful Jonas, and I'd drop everything and follow the man of my dreams wherever he went.'

'Not necessarily. He could stay here.'

'Oh, come on, Lori. Do you seriously think a man like Jonas could ever be happy practising medicine in Bay Beach?'

'Maybe not, but—'

'Or, two,' Em continued ruthlessly, 'we could have a mad, passionate affair, then he leaves, I break my heart, and I sit around for the rest of my life like Miss Haversham in that Charles Dickens novel.'

'What, surrounded by rats and wedding cake?' Her friend eyed her dubiously. 'Unlikely! Bernard would stir himself to eat the cake, and your patients would queue even if you were wearing your fifty-year-old wedding dress. Em, you don't think you could be going overboard here?'

'No.' Em hardened her heart.

'There is a third option,' Lori suggested.

'Which is?'

Robby had fallen asleep in Em's arms. Lori lifted him out, tucked him into his cot and kissed him goodnight. Then she stood back and eyed her friend in concern.

'You could just have fun,' she told her. 'You could just lighten up, have a fling and enjoy yourself. Heaven knows, you deserve it.'

'I—'

'The world won't end if you have an affair,' Lori said sternly. 'And you might just have a very good time. Think about it. Now, go home. I'm sorry, love, but my Raymond's coming to dinner and I need to cook. My time without too many kids in this house is precious, because I intend to have a love life, even if you don't. Love lives are fun. Think about it.'

And with that she kissed her friend on the cheek and propelled her out the door.

Leaving Em thinking about it.

When she walked into the apartment, Jonas was there and, just like Lori, he was cooking dinner.

The sensation was so unexpected that it brought her up short. She stood in the doorway while the smell of steak filled her nostrils and the aura of his presence filled her senses.

'Um…why are you here?' she managed at last, and he threw her a grin over his shoulder.

'I live here. It's the doctors' quarters,' he told her, quite kindly. 'The nurses showed me through. I've unpacked into one of the spare bedrooms, I've introduced myself to your doormat that calls itself a dog and I'm now thoroughly at home. And I'm cooking us both dinner.' Then, at her look of bewilderment, his grin widened. 'I had Lori ring me when you left the home so I knew when to put the steak on. I was starving!'

'So Lori knew?'

'Of course Lori knew,' he told her. 'Otherwise how could I have timed the steak?'

That much was unanswerable. Em thought a few unutterable thoughts about deceiving friends and fought to keep her composure. 'You could have eaten without me.'

'Why? You're not vegetarian, are you?' he asked, his face falling. And then the smile returned. 'But, hey, Lori would have told me, and even if you are it's no matter. I'm starving enough to eat two steaks by myself, and I have a heap of crispy herbed potatoes in the oven.'

'Crispy potatoes…' The aroma throughout the kitchen was wonderful. Almost unbelievable. She stalked suspiciously across the room to the oven and pulled the door wide, but it was just as Jonas had said. There they lay, masses of tiny potatoes, baked golden and mouthwatering, and smelling of rosemary and sage and something she couldn't identify.

'Didn't you believe me?' he asked, wounded, and she struggled to know how to answer him.

'You can cook,' she managed finally, and he lifted his brows in mock indignation.

'Lady, I'm a surgeon. If I can repair a heart valve, I can follow a recipe.'

'It doesn't always follow,' she muttered, thinking of men she'd known in the past.

'Then welcome to the new order.' He motioned to the table. There was a salad, already prepared, and a bottle of wine. 'Sit.'

'I don't drink.'

'Because you're always on call?' He'd guessed it. 'But I'm on call tonight. So sit! And enjoy the novelty.'

So she sat while Jonas piled her plate high with steak and potatoes, and poured her a glass of wine and himself a soda water.

'See?' he said virtuously, sitting down himself. 'I'm in an alcohol-free zone for the night, so you can drink all you want.'

'I'd better not.' No way. Two glasses of wine with this man before her—*and his smile*—and she'd not be responsible for her actions, she thought dazedly. *All this and the man could cook?*

But he was looking toward her dog, who hadn't moved since she'd arrived. Well, why would he? He'd been fed today and there was an hour or so before he had to shift to her bedroom.

'Does Bernard ever move?' he asked, motioning over to where her big red dog lay sprawled under the kitchen sink. Waiting for something to drop. Only if it didn't drop right on his lolling tongue, it'd be wasted. Some things weren't worth burning calories for.

Em shook her head, smiling. 'Does Bernard move? That's like asking if a doormat moves.'

'Oh, I see. You chose him for his scintillating conversation, then.' Jonas grinned, his wide, lazy smile reaching up and lighting his eyes. 'Great. I can see I'll fit right in. A woman who demands a lot from her men...'

She blushed bright pink at that. Good grief! Get the conversation back to medicine, she told herself. That way was safest.

'I...I thought you'd be spending the night with Anna.'

That put a damper on the conversation. Jonas's face

looked shuttered. 'Maybe I should be,' he told her. 'But I'm not wanted.'

'Is she OK?'

'Yes.' He bit into his steak and concentrated on his food, but Em knew it was just a ruse to get his thoughts into order. 'She is,' he said finally. 'She's under control. She's home with her kids, packing and being as normal as possible, while she waits to go into hospital tomorrow.'

'Are you happy to use Patrick?' Em asked.

'He's an excellent surgeon,' Jonas told her, still absently concentrating on his steak. 'When I met him I realised I know him a bit. He's older than me, but we trained in the same hospital. Yeah, I'm happy for Patrick to operate and, what's more important, so is Anna.'

'And he was reassuring?'

'The margins all look clear. The lump itself is less than a centimetre across. He wants to do a lumpectomy and node clearance, but he's pretty confident that nothing's spread.'

'And how does that make you feel?' Em asked.

'Better.' He lifted a potato, examined it—then laid it down on his plate again. 'No,' he told her honestly. 'It doesn't. It makes me feel lousy—I feel so damned out of control.'

There was a long silence, broken only by Bernard's inevitable snoring. They finished eating before either spoke again. Em knew that Jonas needed time to come to terms with today's events. The last thing he needed was idle chatter.

So she finished eating, then cleared and stacked the dishwasher while he sat and stared at the table. And stared some more. But she found she didn't mind the silence. She and Grandpa had never needed to make small talk, and somehow, with Jonas, it felt the same.

Like all the little stuff had already been said...

'Thank you for making dinner,' she said at last, the kitchen cleared and the evening closing in on them. She was bone weary, and he still needed space. She touched his shoulder lightly as she passed. 'Bernard and I are going to bed. Is there anything else you need?'

He looked blindly up at her. 'No.'

'It'll be fine,' she told him. And then she looked across at the phone. 'Ring Anna.'

'What?' He glanced at his watch. 'It's after ten o'clock.'

'You think she'll be sleeping?'

'No, but—'

'Ring her, Jonas,' she said softly. 'I haven't had so much wine that I can't cope here. If she wants you to go, then you go.'

'I told you—I'm on call.'

'If Anna needs you, consider it a call. But ring her.'

He looked at her strangely, his eyes blankly inscrutable. 'I guess you're right,' he said at last.

'I think I am.'

He caught her hand and held it, for a whole fraction of a second. It was a short enough time, but it was enough. Em froze at his touch, and could only draw back in relief when he let her go. If he knew what he did to her...

But for Jonas, the sexual tension simply didn't seem to be there. All his thoughts were on his sister. 'Thank you,' he told her, and gave her a weary smile. 'You're right, of course.'

'I have to be,' Em said, and if her voice dragged a little at the thought, who could blame her? 'I don't have much choice.'

Because, choice or not, the invincible Dr Mainwaring wasn't feeling very invincible at all!

She picked up Bernard, hitched him over her shoulder in a fireman's hold as she'd done every night for ten years, and took her pyjama-bag to bed.

CHAPTER FIVE

EM HEARD him telephone.

She lay in bed and listened to his muted tones, and then she heard the receiver being softly replaced. She half expected him to take his car and leave, but he didn't. Anna must have rejected his offer to come and spend some time with her.

Instead, Em listened to the sounds of him going to bed, in the room right beside hers.

The sensation was so strange it seemed surreal. Jonas Lunn, sleeping in her house!

She'd have to get used to it, she told herself. She might have three months of it.

Whew!

And then came the thought, slipping in when least expected.

Maybe she *could* have an affair!

The thought was like lightning, forking at her out of the darkness. It had been Lori's suggestion.

Lighten up and have an affair? She let the thought drift through her tired mind. Let her sexless, overworked life become, for these short few months, just a little more exciting?

Could she do it?

She wasn't an affair sort of girl.

And Jonas wasn't an affair kind of guy, she told herself crossly into the dark. Especially with the likes of her. Anyone could see he could have just about any woman he wanted.

And as for her... She was plain and unadorned, she thought crossly, and that was the way she liked it. She was built for service rather than decoration.

She was destined to sleep with snoring dogs rather than attractive men.

But today he'd kissed her.

As anyone would have, she told herself even more crossly. He'd been under incredible strain while Anna had had her tests, and he was grateful. So he'd kissed her.

End of story. There was therefore no earthly reason why she should be lying here in the dark, touching her lips and remembering what the feel of Jonas's mouth was like against hers...

Boy, she needed a cold shower. And the man was here for three months!

So get a hold on yourself, she told herself furiously. You're behaving like an idiot. Leave the man alone. Use him professionally but nothing more. Now, shut up, stop thinking crazy thoughts and go to sleep.

Her mind didn't obey orders.

It didn't stop thinking crazy thoughts—and it didn't go to sleep.

It couldn't.

In the next bedroom, Jonas was working overtime in the thinking department as well.

First there was Anna.

Tomorrow she faced the surgeon, and his gut wrenched at the thought of it. Hell, she still felt like a kid to him— his baby sister—and all the reassurance in the world couldn't stop him wanting this to be happening to be anyone else—even to him. He'd want anyone to be facing this rather than Anna.

She wasn't a kid, though, he told himself. Her voice on the telephone tonight had been calm and sure.

'It's OK, Jonas. I've told the children what's happening. I've packed a suitcase for each of them and one for me. No, I don't want you to come back tonight. There's nothing more you can do, so leave me be.'

Leave her be...

He couldn't. He felt sick, doing such a thing, and it felt like his mother's rejection all over again. His mother had walked out on them, and now Anna was pushing him away as hard as she could as well.

She wanted to be as independent as he was himself! As they'd both taught themselves to be.

Damn, he couldn't take much more of this. His family had twisted his emotions since he was tiny, and he hated it.

Which was why it was important to keep the rest of him heart-whole and fancy-free, he told himself in the dark. He needed more involvement—emotional involvement—like a hole in the head.

So why did his confused thoughts keep drifting to Em?

His bed was hard against the wall—her wall. He turned over and surveyed it in the dark. What he desperately wanted was to communicate in some way—maybe tap Morse Code messages in the dark.

He gave a wry smile. She'd think he was crazy if he did.

Was her hair unbraided?

Oh, great, now what was he thinking? He stirred in his bed, easing his long frame around on his too-short mattress. Hell!

Leave Emily Mainwaring alone, he told himself firmly. You play with her and you play for keeps. And the last thing you want in your life is a woman.

But two women were there in his thoughts, and both seemed as needful.

Em and Anna.

His sister and his…

And my temporary partner, he told himself fiercely. My medical partner. Nothing else.

The phone rang at midnight.

Jonas was out in the hall to answer it by the third ring, but Em must have had an extension by her bed. As he lifted the receiver he could hear her already talking, and she'd obviously recognised the voice before the caller had identified herself. Jonas caught the urgency in her tone, and he unashamedly listened in.

'Lori? Is that you?' Em was saying. 'Lori, I can't hear you until you pull yourself together. Take two deep breaths and tell me what's wrong.'

How had she picked up that it was her friend? The voice down the telephone was a terrified series of gasps, and to Jonas it could have been anyone.

But Em was right. It was Lori. There was a sharp intake of breath and then, finally, she made herself coherent.

'Em, it's Raymond. He…he came to dinner and we were watching television. He got up to go and then… Em, he's collapsed and stopped breathing. He's on the floor…'

'Then you know how to do CPR and artificial respiration,' Emily snapped. 'Do it, Lori. Don't think about anything else but keeping him alive. I'll be there in two minutes. Lori, keep your head and move!'

Formula One drivers had nothing on Emily Mainwaring, Jonas decided. He'd hauled pants and a sweater over his pyjamas, and he'd only just reached the car as she gunned it into action. Then they were screaming down the street,

Em's hand flat on the horn to warn oncoming traffic. Her car was making enough noise to waken the dead.

They should be driving his Alfa, Jonas thought grimly, instead of Em's battered sedan. But presumably she had everything she needed packed into her car, and he wasn't arguing. Not that she had time to listen.

And he couldn't get out of her car now—not at the speed she was moving. She hadn't even acknowledged his presence as he'd launched himself into the car, and Jonas knew all her thoughts were on getting to her friend's assistance as fast as possible.

'Can I ring the ambulance?' he asked as her tyres screeched around the first corner. She nodded, her eyes not leaving the road.

'Yes.' She motioned to the cellphone on the console. 'Hit one. Tell them we have a cardiac arrest at Bay Beach Home Two. Maybe I'm wrong, but that's what it sounds like. Then hit three. That'll connect you to the air ambulance. If we pull him around he's going to need critical care and we can't give him that here. They'll fly down from Sydney to collect him. Blairglen's not big enough to support a major coronary care unit.'

'Are you sure we'll need them?' Jonas was lifting the cellphone as he spoke.

'No,' she said grimly. 'Of course I'm not sure. But if we're lucky, we will. Tell them to be on standby anyway—and cross your fingers and toes and anything else you have at the ready.'

'Right.'

But using the cellphone was harder than he'd thought. Em was cornering like her car was on rails—as it definitely wasn't—and Jonas was hurled against the side of the car as she spun.

She wasn't the least sympathetic. 'Tighten your seat

belt,' Em snapped, still not looking at him. 'I can't slow down, and if you hit the door that hard again it could fly open. That's all I need. A road casualty.'

'Yes, ma'am.' Whoops! He tightened his seat belt, ruefully acknowledging that if he'd been hurt it would have been his own stupid fault. Then he concentrated on contacting the ambulances.

Once again, Em's attention was solely on her driving.

And finally he did it. The ambulance radio operators must have heard the desperation in his voice, caused by trying to stay upright in the face of Em's frantic driving. He had no trouble convincing them their need was urgent, and by the time he was finished Em had halted in front of the Bay Beach Home.

And she didn't stop. She didn't even switch off the engine—just left the car standing open at the front door, flung herself out—she was wearing some sort of pale blue jogging suit that she must have worn to bed—and then she was gone.

Hell!

Jonas was accustomed to calls for the crash cart at hospital, and knew the speed with which the staff mobilised. She'd beaten even them, he thought dazedly. They'd have been lucky to have got here faster if Raymond had collapsed in a bed in a ward two floors below them in a major hospital.

He took a little longer than Em to go inside the house, though. He prioritised. Trusting Em to keep Ray's breathing going, he took the time to switch off the engine, open the boot, grab the cardiac gear and follow.

The scene that met his eyes inside was dramatic. Raymond was slumped unconcious on the living-room floor, with Em working furiously on him and Lori looking on. Raymond's face was as grey as Lori's was white.

He must be in total cardiac arrest, Jonas thought, asking no questions and setting the gear up fast. The man was in his late thirties or early forties, and he was definitely portly. He was wearing a business suit. Lori or Em must have hauled his tie away and ripped his shirt open, but he had every appearance of a businessman who'd spent too much time behind his desk and not enough time in the open air.

There was no more time for appraisal. Em looked up from pushing breath into Raymond's chest and saw him. Her face cleared as she saw he was setting up what she needed most, and she moved to make room for him.

'CPR's not working,' she told him. 'Lori can do it like a professional, and she has been, but she's had no response.'

So it was the paddles. A replay of Charlie.

But not with the same results. Please?

They worked hard and fast, with Lori taking over Raymond's breathing, which left the doctors free to work on his chest.

One jerk.

Nothing.

'Come on. Come on!'

It was a prayer, muttered aloud by Em after the second jerk, and then, magically, Raymond's chest heaved of its own accord.

For a moment everyone else in the room stopped breathing. Waiting...

And then there came a searing, ragged gasp that had Lori collapsing in a sodden heap over her boyfriend's chest. 'Oh, Ray. Don't die. Come on, Ray, you can do it.'

'Move back, Lori,' Em said, tugging her friend gently away so the paddles were clear if they needed them again, but there was hope written all over her face. She looked around to find what she needed, but Jonas, once again, was anticipating her needs.

There was oxygen waiting. Once Ray was breathing for himself, they could get on a mask. They could set up an intravenous drip and begin to dissolve the clot with medication.

And they could hope like hell that no long-term damage had been done, and his heart kept right on beating.

There was a siren in the distance, and Em allowed herself to close her eyes for a fraction of a second. She was saying thank you, Jonas thought as he watched her. She was *so* involved with her patients.

Hell!

It was hell. Being a family doctor in a community like this must be just that, he thought. Being involved with every patient you treated…

His own resolution flashed through his head. He'd been hurt so badly in childhood he'd resolved never to become emotionally involved with anyone other than Anna. And here was Em, taking on the heartaches of an entire community.

She'd go crazy, he thought as he watched the conflicting emotions playing over her face. She couldn't keep doing this, year in, year out, for the rest of her life. She'd burn out.

So maybe she was here for the short term—just as he was.

Only he'd go out voluntarily, but she'd go out in a state of near collapse.

Not while he was here, she wouldn't, he vowed. He could at least give her a few months' respite. The only thing was—he had to keep his level of detachment on track.

Which was really, really hard. Like now…

'Stand back for a bit, Em,' he told her, and his voice sounded gruffer than usual, even to him. She needed breathing space to get herself together. Maybe she even needed to do what he suspected she might wish to—as Lori was doing—which was burst into tears.

As an emotional outlet it had a lot going for it, he decided. Strangely, he could use a few tears here himself!

'Go out and radio the air ambulance,' he told Em. 'Tell them to upgrade because the need is urgent.' What they needed here was a cardiologist, and intensive-care facilities. 'Will you go on the plane with him?'

'I can't.' It was an instinctive reaction, but then Em caught herself, thinking it through. Why not? Jonas was here now. She had another doctor to take over! 'I guess I can,' she said slowly. 'If you'll cover me.' She looked ruefully down at her pale blue ensemble, and gave a wry smile. 'Just lucky I go to bed decent. Will you feed Bernard? I'll come back on the train in the morning.'

'Go and pack, Lori,' Jonas said, taking command as if he'd been born to it. 'The hospital will provide gear for Raymond, and more things can be sent on later, but you'll need a change of clothes and toothbrush for yourself. And, yes, Em, of course I'll feed Bernard. It'll be a pleasure to see if he's actually alive.'

But Lori was looking wildly from Raymond to Jonas and then back to Raymond. At that moment, Ray's eyes fluttered open. He saw her, his hand moved feebly and Lori's hand caught his. And the thing was settled.

'You need to go,' Jonas said.

'But there's still Robby,' Lori whispered, her eyes not leaving Ray's. 'The baby…'

Jonas sighed. A dog. A baby. What next? 'I can cope,' he told them both, and he made his voice firm.

Which was more than he felt. He could cope with a dog, he thought, but a baby?

What on earth was he letting himself in for?

Em arrived back at Bay Beach at midday on the following day.

Exhausted from the events of the previous night, she'd slept the entire journey. She woke as the train pulled into Bay Beach station, and when she emerged to daylight she was still feeling fuzzy and confused.

She was even more fuzzy and confused when she saw what was waiting for her on the platform.

Jonas was there, holding baby Robby. And with him were Sam and Matt and Ruby, and behind them, standing up like he hadn't stood up in years, was one woolly Bernard.

Here, then, were Anna's kids, and Em's tiny burns patient. And her dog!

Jonas was standing in their midst like a modern-day Pied Piper. Robby was cradled in the crook of his left arm, looking around him with wide-eyed interest. Four-year-old Ruby was clutching her uncle's spare hand as if her life depended on it, and Matt and Sam, six and eight respectively, looked just plain bewildered. But they were clutching Em's dog in the same way Ruby was clutching her uncle.

Bernard was being useful?

'Hi,' Jonas said as if there was nothing abnormal in this reception in the least. 'Nice train trip?' He smiled at what she was wearing—the plain blue jogging suit he'd sent her off in last night. 'Still wearing your pyjamas, I see.'

Em flushed. 'I don't own pyjamas. They only get me into trouble. And, yes, thank you, I had a very peaceful train trip, which was just what I needed.'

She looked down at the children and then back at him, but he'd stopped smiling and his face was inscrutable. In truth, he was having trouble with his emotions here. She looked so darned pretty—flushed from sleep and slightly dishevelled—and that damned jogging suit *did* look like pyjamas.

Concentrate on medicine, he told himself. Concentrate on the things which were really important. Which didn't include his emotions!

'Ray?' It was a whole medical interrogation in the one word.

'He's still in Intensive Care.' Em's face clouded as she thought of her patient. 'We got him safely to Sydney, but it was just as well I flew with him. He arrested again on the flight. There's been some damage.'

'Neurological problems?' Had they reached him soon enough? Jonas wondered. He'd stopped breathing for about five minutes—long enough for there to be a lack of oxygen to the brain. Long enough for there to be real damage.

But Em was shaking her head. 'There's some heart scarring obvious, but no brain damage that we can see.' Her face lightened with the thought. 'That's the one bright thing in this mess. He's able to talk to Lori, and he knows what's happened. But I suspect he's in for a bypass at the very least.'

She sighed. 'And I did warn him. For as long as I've been practising medicine here, I've been warning him. His cholesterol levels were way too high. He kept coming in for check-ups as if the check-ups themselves might help.'

'And now he's nearly lost everything.'

He had. The thought still made Em's heart twist, and the urge to share it with Jonas was impossible to resist.

She, who normally kept things to herself, found Jonas was a man to confide in. A friend?

Or something more.

'Ray...Ray asked Lori to marry him,' she told him, still taking in the sight of the children and dog around him, and with only half her mind on Lori and Ray back in Sydney. Jonas with children was enough to give any woman pause.

And so was the way he made her feel.

Concentrate on Ray and Lori...

'He proposed half an hour before he collapsed,' she said, and her voice was suddenly shaken with unexpected emotion. 'But Lori knocked him back. She told him her kids came first. He'd brought her an engagement ring. It was in his pocket when he collapsed, and now she's sitting beside him in Coronary Care wearing the damned thing like her life depends on it.'

'Sometimes you have to nearly lose something to realise how much you value it,' Jonas said gravely, and she looked sharply up at him. There was something in his voice that wasn't right. He was under strain, too. Of course.

'Anna?'

'Anna's being operated on as we speak.'

'Oh, Jonas, you should be there with her.'

'I can't be in two places at once,' he told her. He looked down at the kids and managed a smile. 'Can I, kids?' Then, as he got shaky smiles in return, he kept on speaking. 'When Lori left, Anna decided to put off the operation. It was only by giving her my absolute assurance that we'd look after the children that she agreed to go ahead.'

He paused to let this sink in.

'We?' Em said carefully—and waited.

Another pause. And then those dangerous eyes twinkled.

'We have a big house.' He said it sort of hopefully—like an overgrown Labrador puppy might have spoken if it could speak—and Em couldn't help but smile.

'A big house?' she repeated as if she didn't understand what he was getting at. Although she understood only too well, and her heart was sinking. What had he let them in for?

But Jonas was assuming an air of innocence—and of virtue. 'It's a really big house,' he said firmly. 'Far too big for just you and me and Bernard.'

'How did you get Bernard to his feet?' Em asked, fascinated, and Jonas grinned.

'The kids did that. They simply refused to take no for an answer. He's been sighing like you wouldn't believe, but every time he sits down the kids simply hoist him up again.' His smile widened. 'So you see—Bernard needs company.' His smile faded then, assuming an air of uncertainty. 'And I knew you'd want to look after Robby, anyway, Dr Mainwaring. So how could I not offer to look after everyone?'

Everyone. Bernard and Sam and Matt and Ruby.

And Robby.

There was the rub. Em looked at the little boy in Jonas's arms and her heart twisted with pain for him. She was tired and confused. So much had happened. She needed space to think this through.

But Jonas was holding Robby out to her, and he was so little. He'd been so dreadfully injured, and he was so...

So much a part of her!

Help!

She didn't mind offering to take on Anna's children, she thought desperately, and she didn't seem to have much choice about having Jonas in the house, but Robby was a different matter.

Robby was…well, Robby was just Robby.

Which was why she'd discharged him from hospital! Because this little one was bonding to her—and she was bonding right back. And here was Jonas stating calmly that they'd taken responsibility for him.

And for his sister's children as well!

'Have you contacted the head of the orphanage?' she asked cautiously. 'I'd assume their administration will have definite ideas on how Robby's cared for.'

'The other homes are full,' Jonas told her. 'Tom, the homes director, contacted me this morning. He says the only answer is to transfer Robby—and Anna's kids if they need accommodation—to a home in Sydney.'

'No!'

'And I knew you didn't want that,' Jonas said blandly. 'Neither does Robby's aunt. She says cram him into another of the homes, but Tom refused to do that. So I thought if I offered to help you with Robby and Bernard…'

She had him worked out. 'Then I might offer to help you with Sam and Matt and Ruby?'

'That's the one.' He beamed. 'Two days ago there was only one doctor in Bay Beach. Now there's two doctors, but with four kids and a dog between them. Surely we can manage.'

'And your childminding skills would be…?'

'I can build sandcastles,' he said virtuously, and she had to grin.

'How about changing nappies?'

He sniffed at that. And then he sniffed again. 'Uh-oh…'

'Nappies aren't your forte, then, Dr Lunn?'

'That's why we're waiting on the station for you,' he told her generously. 'So you can share.'

'Gee, thanks.'

'Think nothing of it,' he told her and handed over Robby with a promptness that made her chuckle. 'Here's your baby.'

Your baby.

That got to her.

She looked down at Robby, and then she looked up at Jonas. This was dangerous territory they were getting into, she thought—and she wondered if Jonas knew exactly how dangerous it really was.

He had it all worked out.

Back at the house, Em's sometime receptionist, Amy, was waiting for them. The teenager had lunch on the table, and she smiled her welcome as Jonas ushered his brood indoors.

It was some brood. One partner and four children.

And one dog. Bernard made straight for his place under the sink and lay down. Immediately, he had two children tugging him up again.

And Amy was smiling at them all, making Em even more confused. 'Hi.'

'Hi, Amy. What are you doing here?'

'Lou's flu is better.' Amy beamed as if that fact alone was little short of miraculous. The teenager really hadn't enjoyed her short stint as medical rececptionist. 'So Lou's back at Reception and Dr Lunn knew I was out of work. To be honest, I'm happier childminding than I am waiting for someone to vomit all over the waiting-room floor. So when Dr Lunn suggested I be your short-term nanny I thought it'd be cool.'

Cool...

'It fitted perfectly.' Jonas beamed with the satisfaction of a man who'd just put in the final piece of a very complicated jigsaw puzzle. 'Isn't it perfect, Dr Mainwaring?'

'Perfect,' she said faintly, and his smile faded.

'It is. It will work, Em. It must.'

'I can see that.' That it must.

'Amy will be here during the day, and at night only one of us needs to be on call. So the kids can be settled.'

But Em was still holding Robby close. Robby, who had such a hold on her heart...

'Why are you looking afraid?' Jonas asked gently, and she knew that he saw way too much for her liking. He knew her too well. Instinctively he knew what she was thinking, and she found the sensation almost frightening.

'I'm just trying to figure how I can let go of Robby—again,' she murmured, and he looked at her for a long time.

'Maybe you don't want to,' he said at last.

'But—'

'And maybe there's no need.' He reached forward and touched her very lightly on the nose—a feather touch that sent electric currents straight through her. 'Have a think about that. With Amy's help, you don't need to. Meanwhile, if I can leave you with Amy and the kids, I really need to go to Blairglen and see Anna.'

'Of course,' she said.

'This *is* going to work,' he told her strongly. 'If we make it.' He looked at her for a long, long moment, in his eyes a question, but what he saw seemed to satisfy him. He gave a decisive nod.

'OK, kids,' he told his niece and nephews. 'You know what's happening. I'm leaving you to get settled with Dr Em and Amy, but I'll be back tonight to tell you how Mummy is. OK?'

'OK,' they quavered, and Em knew they were as scared as she was.

But, like them, she had no choice.

'Jonas,' she said as he turned away, and he turned straight back to face her.

'Yes?' Their eyes met, and once again that intangible thing passed between them. That thing that scared Em so much...

'Stay as long as you need to tonight,' she told him. 'Amy and I will be fine. Give our love to Anna. And...'

'And?'

'And I have all my fingers and toes crossed for her,' she said simply. 'And anything else I can think of.'

'Thank you,' he said. Their eyes locked above the heads of the four children and once again that silent message was passed.

They may as well have kissed...

CHAPTER SIX

IT WAS midnight before Jonas returned.

Em was wide awake when his car pulled in—not because she needed to be, but because she simply couldn't sleep.

Everyone else was sleeping. There was no reason not to be asleep herself, and no reason why she should be nervous about having the children on her own. Jonas, she discovered, had even provided for night-shift child care.

Amy went home at six but if both doctors were called out, the arrangement was to open the connecting door to the hospital, alert the night staff, and the house could be treated as an extra kids' ward, to be checked by the nurses at need.

It was so simple, Em thought. She just wished her feelings about Jonas were as straight forward.

Not so simple either were her feelings for the little boy in the crib beside her bed. Her bedroom was the logical place for him to be, she'd decided, a decision made even easier by the boys' insistence that Bernard sleep in *their* bedroom, but the reason why her heart turned over at every movement Robby made wasn't logical in the least.

She didn't intend to have babies, she told herself for maybe the thousandth time in her life. So…she couldn't attach herself to Robby. She couldn't!

Just like she was never going to marry. There simply wasn't room in her life for a family.

But she loved—*loved*—the baby sleeping beside her. She could no longer ignore it. And part of her loved the fact that her too-big house was now full of kids and dogs and…

And Jonas.

This was all far, far too complicated!

And now here was Jonas, returning to make her heart do things that were completely foreign to her. Complicating her life still further.

She should stick her head under her pillow and force herself to sleep, she told herself crossly, but she could do no such thing.

Instead, as Jonas's key turned in the lock, she padded through to the living room to meet him.

He was exhausted.

She'd left the wall lamp on in case one of the children wandered in the night. It threw enough light on Jonas's face to show his facial features harshly etched, as if he was deeply exhausted. His eyes were dark and shadowed, and the expression on his face was grim.

'Jonas?' Her heart lurched in fear. Dear heaven, Anna… What had happened?

But he saw her in the shadows, and his face cleared like magic. 'Em.'

'How is it with Anna?'

He'd taken a step toward her—for a moment she thought he was going to reach for her—but the tone of her voice stopped him.

It was meant to. She was getting far too emotionally involved here. She had to stand back a bit.

She couldn't take his proffered hands.

So she made her voice clinical—doctor enquiring of colleague about a mutual patient—and she waited until he pulled himself into order.

'I… She's fine.'

She relented, just a little. 'But you're not fine,' she told him. 'I can see that. Come and have a cup of tea and tell me about it.'

'You couldn't make that a brandy?'

'It went as badly as that?'

'No.' His face twisted into a grimace of a smile. 'Hell, no. It's just that I'm exhausted.' He shrugged. 'I didn't get much sleep last night.'

Of course he hadn't—and at least she'd had the train journey for sleep. Once more, her heart twisted. Somehow she managed to keep her voice dispassionate, but there were still these darned undercurrents running through her. Undercurrents she didn't know what on earth to do with.

She took refuge in practicalities, crossing to the dresser, finding the brandy and pouring him a drink.

Handing it to him was tricky. She had to cross her emotional barrier. Her closeness limit. But then she backed away and hitched herself up onto the dresser, to watch him from a safe distance.

'I won't bite, you know,' he said conversationally, and she managed a smile at that.

'Nope. But I like it here.' She motioned to the armchair. 'Sit down and tell me all.'

He sat, but his eyes didn't leave hers. 'You look like a pale blue, very odd sort of garden gnome,' he complained. 'A garden gnome after a spray-paint job. You don't look doctor-like at all.'

She thought about that, looked down at her jogging suit and smiled. 'Hmm. Don't you approve of the night-time me? Would you like to come through to my surgery while I put on a white coat?'

He grinned. 'That's kinky, Dr Mainwaring. I think I'll leave it like it is. In fact, I kind of like it. Gnome-like instead of doctor-like.'

She smiled again, but then there was silence. Things

settled between them. Almost. Em was still achingly aware of the closeness of him. He was eight feet away. Or, if you looked at it another way, he was three short steps away...

'Tell me about Anna,' she managed, and waited some more.

He looked at her, with that strange, questioning look that told her he only half believed she wanted to know. He wasn't accustomed to professional caring, she thought. He wasn't used to country doctors who worried about their patients on a personal as well as a professional level.

'It's gone as well as it could have,' he told her.

'Which means?' Once more, she waited.

'Small tumour. As the X-rays showed, it's less than a centimetre across. It was all contained in the soft tissue under the breast, and it doesn't look like there's any spread at all. They've taken a fair margin, but there's no sign of dispersion. They haven't had to touch the nipple, so she'll be left with one breast just slightly smaller than the other. If the pathology shows the margins are clear, I doubt Anna will even need a prosthesis.'

'That's great. And the nodes?'

'They've done a complete node clearance. It looks good.' Jonas's face cleared then, but he looked down into the brandy as if he was trying desperately to see into the future. 'One node was slightly enlarged, but we have to wait until late tomorrow or the next day for the pathology results.'

'Oh, Jonas...'

'It's a bloody long wait,' he said.

'Longer for Anna than for you.' But still it was hard for him. Suddenly she could bear it no longer. Slipping off her perch, she took the steps to cross the barrier between them. She placed her hands on the back of his neck and started to massage, slowly, expertly easing the knots of tension across his shoulder blades.

He sighed at her touch, and leaned back into her, but she knew his mind was still on Anna.

'You know, even if it has spread to the nodes, at stage two the prognosis is still positive.'

'I know that.' He shook his head. 'There was someone else there,' he said slowly, and Em thought this through. He sounded so weary it was as if conversation was an effort.

'Waiting to hear how Anna went, do you mean?'

'Yes. Just sitting, like me, waiting to know she'd come out of Theatre.'

Her brow wrinkled. 'Was it Kevin?' She'd thought Anna's de facto husband had long gone.

He shook his head at that. 'No chance. If it had been, I reckon I'd have strangled him with my bare hands. This guy's name is Jim Bainbridge. Big guy. In his late thirties.'

'I know Jim.' Em's hands were still doing their gentle massage and she could feel the knots of tension in Jonas's shoulders slowly unravel. 'Jim's the local fire chief. He's a really nice man. Almost pathologically shy, though.' She thought about it and saw the connection. 'He's Anna's nearest neighbour. They share a back fence.'

'Mmm.'

'You think he's fond of her?'

'I think he looked almost as strained as me. He definitely cares.'

'Well, Jim's not a loser or an alcoholic,' Em said softly, seeing where his thoughts were heading and allaying his fears before he voiced them. 'He's gentle, he's steadily employed and, to my knowledge, he's a one-can-of-beer-after-a-major-bushfire man.'

'Well, that'd be a change.' Jonas sighed again. 'It'd be a big man to take on Anna, though. Three kids and breast cancer...'

That made Em pause. Her hands stilled. 'You mean you don't think Anna has anything left to offer?' she asked quietly. 'Just because she's lost a piece of her breast?'

'I didn't mean that. Of course I didn't mean that.' Jonas's face creased into a weary smile, and his hands came up and caught hers over his shoulders. 'I only meant...well, three kids are a handful, and on top of that she's running scared.'

'Just like you.'

'I'm not scared.'

'Of relationships?' Her hands broke away from his and went back to kneading. 'Of needing people? Pull the other leg, Jonas Lunn.'

Silence.

'I'm not, you know,' he said conversationally, as though it had only just occurred to him.

'Scared of relationships?'

'That's right.'

'So you're aching to fall in love, right at this minute.'

'I could be tempted,' he said, and the warmth in his voice gave her pause. 'For instance, if you said right now that you'd come to bed with me...'

'You'd have your packet of condoms out quicker than I could say wedding ring,' she said bluntly, and she couldn't quite keep the bitterness out of her voice. 'That'd be right. Only it's not going to happen. Neither of us will say bed, you won't say condoms, and I won't say wedding ring. Because it's not what either of us wants.'

'You don't necessarily,' he said carefully, 'have to take bed, condoms and wedding ring as a job lot. They can be separated.'

'What, go to bed with you without a condom?' She raised her eyebrows in mock indignation. Still she kept on massaging. It was a link she didn't want broken, condoms or not. 'Gee, thanks very much. We have four kids here already. You're saying let's make it five?'

'I meant the marriage thing,' he told her. He put her hands away, rose and twisted to face her, his eyes suddenly serious. He placed his hands on her shoulders, forcing her to meet his gaze. 'Enough.' His eyes were locked on hers, and they were suddenly deadly serious. 'Em, you need to know that I'd like to make love to you. Very, very much.'

And she didn't?

She wanted to make love with Jonas more than anything in the world, she thought wildly. She wanted him to wrap her in those strong arms, to hold her against his chest, to lift her into bed and make her believe...

Make her believe for a few magic minutes that she was young and desirable, and free to make any choice she wanted in life.

But that was the way of madness.

Because at the end of all this, when Anna no longer needed him, he'd walk away without a backward glance.

And his next words confirmed it.

'Em, there's no need for you to look like you're being asked to commit for life here,' he told her. 'For heaven's sake, how old are you?'

'Twenty-nine.'

'And I'm thirty-three. That's old enough to know we can take pleasure where we find it.'

'And walk away afterwards.'

'That's right.'

'Except it doesn't work like that,' she told him sadly,

reality crashing back where it belonged. 'Like me and Robby.'

'I don't understand.'

'I thought I could just love Robby for a little bit,' she said, and her voice was bleak. 'So I let myself become...involved. And now I've got it hard. The full bit. Because, as well as Robby needing me, I need him. I love him, Jonas. That's what love is. Needing, and being needed in return. So now here he is, sleeping in the cot beside me, and the longer it goes on the more it'll tear my heart out when he leaves.'

'I didn't know you felt like that.' He frowned. 'Where's your professional detachment, Dr Mainwaring?'

'I don't have any.' She took a deep breath and pulled back from him. 'You seem to have it in spades but I don't have my share. And it's not fair. Because for you it's no problem.'

'I don't know what you mean.' He was frowning.

'You could have a wife and a family any time you want,' she said, and his brow snapped down again.

'I don't want.'

'Exactly.' She dug her hands into the pockets of her capacious sleeping trousers and met his look full on. 'But I do. I always have. A family would be...wonderful. But I also want to be Bay Beach's doctor. The two together are impossible.'

'You could marry a local,' he said, thinking it through. 'And adopt Robby.'

'Oh, yes?' She jeered. 'How could I do that? What man would take me on, when he'd know I'm on call twenty-four hours a day, seven days a week? You might be able to find a wife who'd live with you on those terms, but male-female roles haven't changed so much that I could find a husband who'd live with it. There's not a snowball's chance in a bushfire of me forming a long-term relationship.'

'Are things here so tough?'

'They are,' she said bluntly. 'This town's big enough for two doctors, and there aren't enough doctors in the neighbouring towns. So I'm it. I'm overworked, I love my job but it allows me no time at all for anything else.'

'Even for Robby?'

She tilted her chin at that. 'There is nothing in the world I'd like more than to adopt Robby,' she told him, and the words confirmed it even to herself. 'For some reason I've fallen for him in a big way. I want him so badly I ache with it. But what sort of mother would I make?'

'I think you'd make a fine one.'

'Yeah, here for thirty minutes of every day and that thirty minutes interchangeable depending on the demands of my patients.' His incomprehension was making her angry. 'Robby would be brought up by a nanny. Amy, maybe? Until she finds a better job? No! He's much better off being adopted by someone who can love him to bits—who can be a real mother to him.'

'But his aunt won't hear of adoption.'

'She will. Eventually she must.'

'And meanwhile you keep tearing your heart out.'

'I wouldn't be tearing my heart out if you hadn't offered for us to look after him.'

'I'm sorry about that, Em,' he told her gently. 'I hadn't realised. But, then, if I hadn't offered he'd be in Sydney and you'd still be aching for him.'

'Yes, well…' The gentleness in Jonas's tone was almost her undoing. Em felt the moisture welling behind her eyes and gave a defiant sniff. 'You weren't to know.'

'I do now.'

'There's nothing to be done.'

'Except live with it,' he said softly. 'I guess you're right. As we need to live with this whole damned arrangement. Me and you and our four kids.'

'And walk away at the end of it?' Her voice was hopeless.

'Yes. With great memories, though.' He caught her shoulders and he looked deep into his eyes. His hold was firm and strong—the hold of a man claiming his own.

But, of course, he wasn't.

'Wonderful memories,' he said softly. 'Em, we both know this is transient—I have a world to go back to when I know Anna has recovered—but we can make it so good for now. We can give the kids a really good time. And…'

'And?' But she knew what he was about to say before he said it.

He said it, just the same. 'Em, I think you're one special lady. Sure, I'm not a man who puts down roots—I never will be—but that doesn't stop me forming relationships if the lady's special enough. And I really would like to sleep with you.'

She flinched. 'I suppose I should feel flattered.'

'No.' He was watching her dispassionately. 'Because you want the same thing. I can feel it.'

'No!'

'Go on.' His eyes mocked her. 'Say you don't want it.'

'I don't want it.'

'Liar.' His hold tightened and suddenly there was a link between them that was growing stronger by the minute. It was the silence, she thought desperately. It was the warmth of the big, old house. The knowledge that there were four children sleeping in their care…

It was a setting that felt so sweet it made Em want to weep, and the more she looked up at this man the more she found it impossible to pull away.

'Em…' His eyes were searching hers, seeking an answer which she didn't have the strength to give.

She should pull away. She should whisk herself back to her bedroom and lock the door behind her, leaving Jonas to watch her go.

But she could no sooner do it than fly. The link between them was way, way too strong.

He released her shoulders and his hands cupped her face. His fingers were tracing the paleness of her throat, pushing her face gently up to meet his.

And then there was a long, long silence—a silence where things were built and not broken. Where things were said that could never be said aloud.

Where things were joined that couldn't lightly be put asunder.

Their eyes stayed locked. There was confusion in both of them—uncertainty—a lack of knowledge of the future—but for now, right at this moment, there was only each other.

And then he kissed her.

Em had been kissed before.

Of course she'd been kissed before. She was twentynine, she'd had a normal fun life as a medical student and even after she'd come back to Bay Beach there'd been men who'd fancied their chances with Dr Emily. They hadn't wanted the baggage of the workload that went with her but, intermittently, they'd wanted her.

So she'd been kissed.

But not like this!

This was a kiss that she hadn't believed was possible. It was the joining of two halves of a whole, she thought desperately as the warmth from Jonas's mouth flooded through her body, warming her from the tip of her toes to the top of her head.

Warming her?

It was the wrong description. This was like resuscitation, she thought dazedly. It was like bringing the dead back to life.

Until this moment she'd never known she could feel like this, and the sensation was indescribable.

His lips claimed hers. Their mouths held and locked. Jonas's arms were around her, crushing her breasts to his chest, and she was melting into him like this was her natural home.

Man and woman—meeting and merging. Becoming one.

The sweetness was indescribable. It was threatening to overwhelm her. The feeling that here at last was her place in the sun. Her man...

Only he wasn't her man. He was Jonas Lunn, city surgeon, and in a few weeks he'd be away from here for good. He'd love her and leave her, and she'd have to get on with her dreary existence without him.

Her hair would have to stay braided.

So when his hand went to the base of her braid and she felt him twist the tie, wanting to free her mass of hair, the sensation made her pull away in instinctive self-defence.

'No!'

'Yes,' he said, and his gorgeous eyes mocked hers. 'You want this, Emily Mainwaring. You know it. You want this as much as I do.'

'Maybe I do,' she said honestly, meeting his eyes with candour. 'But maybe I have enough sense to see where it would lead.'

'It would lead to two people taking comfort in each other—that's all.'

'And then you'd walk away?'

'Yes,' he said honestly. 'Of course I would. And life would keep going, but it'd be the richer for our joining.'

'No, it wouldn't, Jonas,' she said, and her voice was tight with strain and bleakness. 'It'd be dreadful. Like me losing Robby now. I'd break my heart.'

'You don't lose your heart by going to bed with some-one.'

'No?' She glared at him. Men! Were they all this in-sensitive? 'How else do you lose it?'

'I guess you don't lose it at all,' he said uneasily. 'At least, I don't.'

'Lucky you.'

'Em, this is hardly World War Three. Do you have to be so dramatic?'

'I'm not being dramatic.' She was really angry now. What had he said?

That doesn't stop me forming relationships if the lady's special enough...'

How many *special* ladies had he walked away from?

Well, one of them wasn't going to be her, she decided, and it was her anger that finally pulled her through. It gave her strength. Heavens, she had enough on her plate, worrying about Robby and the medical needs of Bay Beach, without tying herself in knots over this man.

'Go to bed, Jonas,' she told him.

'With you?'

'Your bedroom door's thataway. And my bedroom's in the other direction. So take yourself off and leave me alone. I don't want you.'

'Liar.'

'I may be a liar but I'm lying for the best,' she told him bluntly. 'Whereas your way wreaks havoc for every-one. And I'm starting to see why Anna holds herself back from you. You're detached and independent and you don't give yourself at all.'

'I give—'

'You give your time, your money and your work. But not yourself, Jonas. And it's not enough. You want to be needed, but you won't need in return. It's not enough for Anna, and it's not enough for me. Goodnight!'

She walked into her bedroom and slammed the door behind her. Hard.

How could she sleep after that?

She lay in the dark and listened to Robby's gentle snuffling, and her heart cried out for what could never be.

A baby and a man. A man and a baby.

Her two impossible loves.

In the adjoining room, Jonas did the same. He lay in the dark and let the events of the last twenty-four hours unfold around him.

Anna. Anna pushing him away. 'I don't need you. I don't need anyone,' she'd said as he'd offered to stay into the night.

And Em...

'You give your time, your money and your work. But not yourself...'

What was a man to do?

He was just trying to do what was right, he told himself bleakly. He'd come down here because Anna needed him, whether she knew she did or not. And Em... She needed him too, emotionally as well as for her precious medicine.

So why couldn't they just let him give what he was able to?

Because he'd walk away.

It was the truth. He knew it, and he'd acknowledged it openly. Anything else would be dishonest.

He wouldn't make love to Em under false pretences. He didn't *need* her. He didn't *need* anyone.

But he wanted to make love to Emily so much that it hurt.

Hell!

The children were out of bed before he was, and his first waking thought was that a ten-ton weight had landed on his chest. But no. It was just three children.

'Wake up, Uncle Jonas. Em's making toast, even Bernard's awake and we asked Em how Mum was but she said to ask you. So we came in to ask.'

Three little faces peered at him with varying levels of anxiety, and he relented enough to gather as many arms and legs as he could into a together bear-hug. It felt strange—but good.

These were his niece and nephews. He'd never been allowed close but they, it seemed, didn't have the reservations their mother had.

'Your mum came though the operation fine,' he told them. 'If everything goes well the ambulance will bring her back to the Bay Beach Hospital tomorrow, so you'll be able to see her then for yourselves.'

They'd arranged that already. They could have transferred her today, but Anna wanted to be away when the test results came through. She wanted time out without the children, to come to terms with everything that had happened to her.

And to prepare herself for the worst, if the worst was likely.

Please, let it not be, Jonas said silently, and told himself again that there was no reason to think that it should come to the worst.

Cancer. What was the medical saying? That it was a word. Not a sentence...

He forced his attention back on the kids. 'Did you say Em's making toast?'

'Yep. She's just got back. There was a farmer who got his foot crushed when a cow stood on him.' That was Sam. 'So when we woke up, one of the nurses was here and she told us to be very quiet until you woke up. But then Em came back and said you were a lazy-bones so we could come and wake you up all we liked.'

'Isn't Em wonderful?' He grinned and threw back the covers, but a part of him felt guilty. She'd been out working while he'd slept. She'd organised a nurse to check the kids so he could sleep on.

She had the phone beside her bed, he thought. Another was in the hall, but if she answered on the first ring he wouldn't hear it.

That'd have to be changed.

But the kids were focusing on breakfast. 'There's three sorts of jam,' Ruby told him earnestly. 'Em's got strawberry jam and raspberry jam and marmalade, and Bernard likes marmalade best, and Robby's got strawberry jam all over his face.'

'I bet he has.'

'Come on, Uncle Jonas.'

'Wait until I get dressed.'

'The toast's ready now!' And, like it or not, his pyjama-clad figure was towed forth into the kitchen.

Em was there, and the sight of her made him...well, it sort of set him back.

It wasn't a shock, exactly. She was looking the same as she had the day before. It was just that she was holding baby Robby in her arms and was chuckling at the mess he'd made, and Bernard, amazingly, was on his feet, whuffling around for more toast. Em was surrounded by domesticity and chaos.

It was nothing he couldn't recover from, he told himself harshly. Given time.

And a bit of distance.

It wasn't to be. Robby was thrust into his arms like he was expected to take a dual parenting role. 'I need a face-cloth,' Em told him. 'Urgently. Take a kid while I find one.' Then she looked him up and down. 'By the way, I love your pyjamas.'

They were silk. They also had very cute pandas all over them. A gift from a lady friend…

Hell, he almost felt like blushing.

The kids were giggling, too. 'We didn't think uncles would wear pandas on their pyjamas,' Ruby said seriously, and Jonas swooped her up in his spare arm. So he had two kids in hand.

'There's nothing this uncle can't do,' he told her grandly.

'Changing nappies?' Em teased, and he winced.

'It's a learned skill,' he told her. 'As a surgeon, I've just learned to apply sticking plasters. It takes years and years of practice before I can graduate to nappies.'

'Plus a bit of raw courage thrown in for good measure.' She was laughing at him, and the sight unnerved him. She was so…

Gorgeous.

Em was gorgeous, he told himself as she attacked Robby with a facecloth. She was dressed for practicality, in jeans and T-shirt, her hair was drawn back into its customary severe braid, she wore not a touch of make-up—and she was gorgeous!

He wanted her so badly...

For now.

And she wouldn't let him near because he'd hurt her long-term.

She had to be the judge of that, he told himself as he settled down to breakfast, surrounded by kids and chaos. No means no. The lady doesn't want you, Jonas Lunn. You'll complicate her life, and the last thing you want is to complicate anyone's life.

Isn't it?

Hmm.

CHAPTER SEVEN

ROSE'S test results came back late that day, and they were magnificent. Jonas drove back from Blairglen feeling like he'd been handed the world.

He pulled in just as Em arrived back from afternoon surgery, and his mood lightened even further at the sight of her. He wanted to shout his good news at the top of his lungs—and who better to share it with than Emily?

But there was someone else—a man—waiting in the shadows of the front porch. He had the look of someone who had waited a long time and was prepared to wait longer. And Jonas recognised him from the day before. It was Jim—the fire chief. The man who'd shared his vigil.

He needed to share his good news with him as well as Em, he thought, but it was such fantastic news that he didn't mind who he shared it with.

As long as Em was included...

She was walking toward him from the surgery side of the hospital and he felt like striding forward, sweeping her up into his arms and whirling her round and round until he was dizzy.

But Jim was waiting, and the expression on his face was desperately anxious.

'I hope you don't mind me coming,' Jim said. The man was visibly sweating. 'I've been phoning all day, but the hospital won't tell me anything. Jonas...mate... I need to know.'

This big, gentle man had sat all through yesterday without seeing Anna, Jonas thought, coming to terms with this new dimension in his sister's life. They'd stayed in the waiting room together, but Jonas had been permitted to go in as Anna had emerged from the anaesthetic. Jim hadn't even had that much comfort.

Still Jim had waited. And today it didn't take a genius to figure that he'd worried himself sick.

Jonas looked sideways at Emily, whose face had softened in understanding.

'You love Anna,' she said gently on a note of discovery, and the man's face grew even more strained.

'She's a great lady. Doc, I can't bear it if anything happens to her.'

'It won't,' Jonas said, and he could contain himself no longer. His voice was exultant. Damn, he wanted to spin *someone*! If he couldn't spin Em, he was almost tempted to spin the fire chief!

'The results are great,' he told them. 'The margins around the lump are clear. The nodes are all negative. It's looking more and more like it's been caught before it can do any damage. There's more tests to be done to confirm things, but at this stage it's looking fantastic.'

Jim's face went slack with relief.

'Oh, that's… Great news. The best.' The fire chief backed away from them, as if it was suddenly necessary to get away—to take on the news by himself. 'It…it…'

His face crumpled and he fled.

Which left Em and Jonas, and Jonas was grinning like a goofy schoolboy who'd just been made class monitor. He still had the urge to spin. But then Em was standing on tiptoe and giving him a tiny kiss, right on the lips— and suddenly he didn't feel like a schoolboy any more.

It wasn't a huge kiss. Maybe it wasn't even a kiss for noticing—but it was one he noticed all the same. He noticed very much!

'I've already heard the news,' she told him. 'I came home as soon as I could. It *is* fantastic.'

'How the heck do you know?' He pulled back, puzzled, and she gave him a wry look.

'Anna is my patient, clever-clogs. I had Pathology ring the results straight through to me as soon as they knew. If the results had been bad I would have driven up to Blairglen to see Anna, but I figured you and Patrick could explain these results to her all by yourselves. They're wonderful.'

Em would have come up...

Of course she would. Because she cared.

Jonas's shoulders went slack from relief—or from exhaustion—or maybe from a mixture of emotions so great he could hardly fathom them.

What was happening here? he asked himself. He normally kept so cool. So distant. He'd learned early to be dispassionate, but here he was, a grown man, and all he wanted to do was burst into tears.

'They haven't graded the tumour yet,' Em was saying, watching him with a strange look on her face. 'Or seen whether it's hormone receptor positive or not. But Patrick seems to think it's cause for celebration.'

'He's pretty sure it's grade one.'

'Well, he saw it, and he's good,' she reassured him. 'I'd expect that Patrick's gut reaction is right. And if he is, that probably means she'll choose no chemotherapy. Just radiation to mop up anything that might have been left, a tiny silicone insert fitted into her bra to make both sides match, and Anna can get on with her life.'

But Jonas was still struggling with mixed emotions. 'Thank...thank God,' he managed, and it sounded inane even to him.

'And it's the same for you, too,' she said gently, watching his face. 'You can go back to being Jonas Lunn, independent surgeon.'

'In three months,' he said shortly. 'After she's had radiation.'

'She'll let you help her for that long?'

'She'll need help while she has the radiotherapy,' Jonas said. 'She must accept it. How will she cope alone?'

'There's a daily bus to Blairglen for radiotherapy.'

'Oh, great. Two hours there, two hours back, every day for seven weeks. She needs to stay at Blairglen.'

'Maybe you could rent a house for all of you,' Em said slowly, still watching the gamut of emotions running over his face and sensing his confusion. 'Take the kids. Stay with her.'

'As if she'd let me do that.'

'You could try.'

'And how about you?' His emotions still weren't totally focused on Anna, no matter how much Em tried to direct them that way. 'How will you cope?'

'Like I always have,' Em said carefully. 'Alone. Nothing's changed for me, Jonas.'

'But there's Robby.'

Her face closed, and he saw pain wash over it. 'Yes,' she conceded. 'There's Robby. But Lori will be back soon. The news from Sydney is good. Ray's on the list for an emergency bypass. It'll be a few weeks before Anna is ready for radiotherapy, so maybe... Maybe you could stay here until then. Until Lori comes back, I mean. That way I can look after Robby for a bit longer, and I don't need to depend on Amy so much.'

'I'll do that.' His face softened. 'You know I'll do that. Hell, Em, I feel so damned good about all this. I feel like...'

She smiled at the joy behind his words. He'd been worried sick and it was obvious. 'Celebrating?' she suggested, and he grinned.

'I think that's the word.' He glanced at his watch. His stomach was telling him it was time to eat, and his stomach was right. 'How about I take you out for a meal?'

'Hmm.'

His brow snapped down at that. He wasn't accustomed to women reacting to his invitations with noncommittal grunts. 'What does "hmm" mean?'

'"Hmm" means you've forgotten your responsibilities, Dr Lunn,' Em said demurely. 'Amy's due to go home, and we need to feed and care for our four children.'

'But—'

'No buts. It's called responsibility.'

He glowered but, damn, she was right. Of course she was right. He'd offered to take care of these kids, and now he had to live with the consequences.

Which meant that he couldn't ask a lady for a date without asking four kids along as well. Unless he changed ladies.

Which, for some inexplicable reason, seemed impossible.

'It'd better be fish and chips on the beach, then,' he said weakly, and she grinned.

'Wise choice.' She motioned to the beeper on her belt. 'As long as this doesn't go off.'

'It'd better not.' He squared his shoulders and readjusted his concept of a perfect date. 'It won't. It's a magnificent night, we've just had some wonderful news, and we deserve an absolutely fantastic meal. All of us. What do you say, Dr Mainwaring?'

What did she say?

Em knew what she ought to say. She ought to say she would have a quiet meal at home with Robby, while Jonas took Anna's children to the beach. She ought to insist they stay separate.

But the thought of what he was inviting her to was insidious in its sweetness. A family meal on the beach. Jonas and herself and four fabulous kids.

How could she refuse an offer like this?

How could she refuse a man like Jonas?

It was, indeed, a magical night.

Fish and chips had never tasted so good. Reassured as to their mother's well-being, and becoming more accustomed to Em and their uncle by the minute, the children set out to enjoy themselves. The summer sun had lost its sting but it had left behind enough heat to make the beach wonderful, and they ended up sitting right at the water's edge, individual bags of fish and chips balanced soggily on their knees as the waves washed over their toes.

Even Bernard was there and, to Em's amazement, he was hopping in and out of the waves and running eagerly back and forth to be fed chips by the kids, with all the energy of a pup!

'Maybe he's been missing children,' Em said wonderingly. 'All these years…maybe he's been seriously depressed and we hadn't figured out why. But look.' Sam fed him a chip and his great red tail wagged like a flag. 'He just needed a family!'

A family. A sweetly insidious thing…

'How can life get better than this?' Em said happily. 'Look out, Ruby. This wave's a big 'un. It'll get your dinner.'

Ruby squealed and raised her fish and chip parcel high—then went happily back to eating until the next wave.

Em was doing an even trickier balancing act. She was

bouncing Robby on her knee, while trying to keep her own fish and chips dry.

'It's not going to work,' Jonas told her, grinning as he watched her. 'Go up past the high-water mark, Dr Mainwaring. It's the only way you can cope. Plus it'll keep Robby's dressings dry. It'll take you half an hour to change them if he gets wet.'

In fact, it'd help him as well. He was having trouble concentrating. Em was wearing a really simple black bathing costume. It shouldn't have the power to do anything to him, but the sight of her in it...

Well, it was enough to put a hungry man off his fish and chips. And right onto something else!

'In your dreams,' she retorted. 'Robby loves the sea—don't you, Robby?' Right on cue, the baby squealed in delight to confirm it. 'And I do, too. If you knew how much I've been longing to be near the sea all day...'

'Then let me help you.' And before she knew what he was about, he'd taken her fish and chips from her. As she lifted Robby from wave to wave, letting his toes just touch the foam and watching him chuckle and chuckle some more, Jonas proceeded to feed her. A chip at a time. One for him, then one for her.

The action was weirdly intimate. Like a joining...

Robby chortled and bounced on Em's knee—his bandages were getting wetter and wetter, but Em refused to worry because surely this amount of joy warranted the trouble of changing them—and the sensation Em felt was indescribable.

Totally indescribable.

She looked around at the kids and the baby and Jonas, a wave broke over her bare toes, Jonas popped another chip into her mouth and for a moment she thought she might cry.

Which was just stupid. Stupid!

'I...I should go home,' she said weakly as the last chip went the way of its counterparts. 'There's work—'

'Your phone hasn't rung.'

'I have so much medico-legal work to catch up on, it's coming out my ears.'

'I'll help you with it after the kids go to bed,' Jonas said promptly, and that caused an even greater wave of sensation to break over her. The thought of this man sitting up with her into the night, ploughing through her mass of paperwork...

'You don't need to do that.'

'I want to,' he said gently, popping a last chip into her mouth, and before she knew what he was about he'd leaned over and lifted Robby into his arms. 'OK, guys. Sam, Matt, Ruby! Collect every single bit of rubbish, take it over to the bin over there and come back. This instant.'

'Why?' asked Sam, ever the suspicious one. He had his uncle's red hair and green eyes, and Em had to grin at the sight of him. Sam was just like Jonas would have looked like at eight years old, she thought. He was so cute.

'Because we're going swimming, of course,' Jonas told him. 'All of us. And anyone who doesn't gets spiflicated.'

They gazed, round-eyed. No one knew what the word meant, but it sounded delicious.

And then Sam tilted his chin.

'You wouldn't dare.'

'Want to not come swimming and find out?'

The boy's face split into a grin.

'Nope,' he confessed.

'Then what are we waiting for? Let's go!'

And Em was left sitting in the shallows, watching as

Jonas and the children splashed and yahooed and chortled and wallowed.

With Robby safely tucked in Jonas's arms, the rest of the children were growing braver and braver—and venturing deeper and deeper.

As was Em.

She was falling deeper in love by the minute!

By the time they had the kids settled into bed it was almost ten o'clock. Em emerged from giving Robby his last bottle to find Jonas sorting things on her desk.

'What do you think you're doing?' she asked, startled, and he grinned.

'Making room for both of us. But I'd change first if I were you.' He looked virtuously down at his showered self, and his clean linen shirt and tousers. He'd showered with the boys. In contrast, Em, who'd had to bath Robby, reapply his bandages, take him through his stretches and give him his last bottle, was still dressed in her bathing suit, her only other covering being a sarong casually twisted around her waist.

She looked lovely, he thought. Just gorgeous! But he couldn't work with her!

'I don't see myself working beside you like that,' he told her.

'I don't see you working beside me at all,' she said, in a voice that was way firmer than she felt. 'It's *my* paperwork.'

'We're partners.'

'You don't know anything about my patients.'

'I can do medico-legal work with my hands tied,' he told her. He gestured to the computer. 'I have the lawyers' letters. Courtesy of your computer, I have your patient notes. We have my laptop. We can look up your notes, you can decide what we can say and I can edit it and type it as we go. Now—any arguments?'

None at all, Em thought, and looked at the mound of solicitors' letters. This pile had been building up to insurmountable levels. It seemed that for every second patient she saw there was an insurance claim or motor-accident form to complete.

And the thought of sharing it was tantalising.

'Just shower, though.' Jonas's voice was gruff. 'I'm not sitting beside you like that, or I won't answer for the consequences.'

And neither would she. She looked down at her bare toes, she looked across at Jonas's laughing face—and she fled.

Because she didn't trust herself in the least. Not one bit!

There was a problem.

Her hair.

Em normally washed her hair once a week. It was a thick, woven mane, it took hours to dry and she had to unbraid it to wash it.

She didn't want to wash it now.

But it was full of sand and salt and, she suspected, the odd bit of baby food where Robby had grabbed it with glee.

'I should cut it off,' she told the mirror crossly. 'It's stupid vanity to wear it like this.'

But her grandpa had loved it, and so had Charlie.

And so did she.

'So wash it and blow-dry it,' she suggested to herself.

'That'll take an hour and Jonas is waiting. He's doing *your* work.'

So she did what she had to do. She unbraided her hair,

she washed it and combed it through, then slipped into her gnome-pyjamas and made her way back to the living room with her hair unbraided.

Jonas was on his feet before she was two feet into the door. He stared—and then he whistled, causing Em to blush from the toes up.

'There's no need for you to whistle,' she snapped. 'I'm still gnome-like. I'm just hairier.'

'I like hairy gnomes,' he told her, and his eyes told her that he spoke the truth. He did indeed like hairy gnomes. Very much indeed!

She flicked the hair away from her shoulders, an action which was nearly his undoing. Wow! But her voice was matter-of-fact and businesslike. 'Come on. If you insist on doing this, let's start.'

'Your hair is still dripping.'

'Let it drip!'

'Let me towel it for you.'

'Jonas Lunn, if you so much as come within two feet of me, I'll scream and run,' she told him crossly, and his green eyes twinkled with mischief.

'What, scared of me, Dr Mainwaring?'

'Yes,' she said honestly.

His smile faded. 'There's no need to be.'

'On the contrary, there's every need to be. You're messing with my equilibrium, and I sometimes think that my equilibrium is all I have to keep me sane. So let's cut out the personal stuff and get on with my letters.'

'Yes, ma'am.'

And that was that.

Somehow he had to ignore the fact that he was sitting by the most desirable woman he'd ever met in his life and get on with work.

Some time soon she'd unbraid her hair just for him,

he thought—and wondered how the heck he could achieve it.

Somehow, the distraction of Em's hair aside, they did it. They worked for two hours straight, setting up a rhythm that had Em's pile descending at a rate she wouldn't have thought possible. Every time she demurred and told Jonas to go to bed, he told her kindly where to get off and lifted another letter from the pile.

She shouldn't let him. But he could sleep in tomorrow, she told herself, and the idea of finishing this paperwork was irresistible.

And then Robby woke.

He was a restless baby. His healing skin itched, and if he turned in his sleep sometimes he hurt himself and woke with a little cry. He wasn't a cry-baby, though. He'd wake, sob a little to himself, and then just lie in his cot and wait for things to get better.

It was as if he knew he didn't have a mother to hold him close, so it was no use making a fuss, and Em couldn't bear it. She was up and in to find him before his second murmur, carrying him back to where Jonas sat working.

'What's the problem?' Jonas pushed his papers away. They really had done enough, and he was ready for bed.

'I don't know.' Em cradled the little boy to her, and her gorgeous hair swung across her back in a shimmering mass. 'I wish he could tell me, but you can't, can you, sweetie? He's wet, but that doesn't usually wake him. Still, now he's up...' She laid him on the settee and set about changing him, then cradled him to her again and turned to find Jonas watching.

'I wish you wouldn't do that,' she complained, and he blinked.

'Wouldn't do what?'

'Stare. Robby and I aren't tourist attractions.'

'You should be. You're gorgeous,' he said bluntly, and it was all she could do not to throw a cushion at him. Honestly, the man had the capacity to knock her sideways.

She fought for composure, and found it finally as Robby snuggled into her.

'No,' she said, and there was a trace of emotion in her voice. 'It's Robby who's gorgeous. Not me. Do you want to hold him?' And before he could refuse she'd popped the baby on his knees and was heading for the kitchen. 'I need a hot chocolate, and I dare say you could do with one, too. And I'll make another bottle to settle Robby again. Take care of Robby while I make them.'

But it was an excuse for her to get away from him, if only for a moment. For her to find her equilibrium again. Somehow.

Jonas was so dispassionate, she thought as she prepared the mugs of chocolate and Robby's bottle. He'd help Anna and then he'd head back out of his sister's life. And she knew that, given half a chance, he'd make love to her, and then he'd leave without a backward glance.

It wasn't enough, she thought. He needed to see that there was more to life…

That there was more to loving than being needed. It was needing in return.

And Jonas Lunn didn't need anyone!

If only he could see what he was missing out on!

When she returned to the sitting room, some of the work had been done. Robby was lying on Jonas's knees. The baby was chortling up at him with his own brand of baby humour, laughing at some joke only an eight-month-old baby could understand, and Jonas looked like a man who'd been struck by lightning.

He glanced up at her as she returned, and somehow he forced his face back under control, but Em could see that Robby had spread some of his indefinable charm.

'He's…he's quite a baby,' Jonas said, and if his voice was a trifle unsteady, Em could pretend she hadn't heard.

'He is at that.'

'Why did you say his aunt doesn't want him?'

'She has three of her own.'

'It wouldn't stop me,' Jonas said, and his voice was suddenly so fierce that Em blinked. 'I mean…if he was my sister's kid.'

'Of course,' Em said kindly, but she looked at him and wondered whether he really meant it. She glanced down again at Robby. Robby was crooning his own happy little song, and his tiny hands were folded in Jonas's much bigger ones.

There was magic going on here tonight, Em thought, but she didn't say a word.

'You want me to give him his bottle?' she asked.

'No.' Jonas's voice was strangely gruff. 'I'll do it. Finish your chocolate.'

'Yours'll get cold.'

'It doesn't matter.'

And it didn't. Em sat and sipped her chocolate, and watched Jonas tenderly feed Robby his bottle, and she found her precious equilibrium slipping further and further from her grasp.

Until it was gone for ever, like it or not.

Anna was transferred by ambulance to Bay Beach Hospital the next day. Em checked her on arrival, ensured she had adequate pain relief and watched as she nestled down against her pillows in relief.

'I'll send you your brother,' she told her as Anna settled

down to sleep. She touched her lightly on her hair, in a gesture of reassurance. 'The ambulance ride will have stirred up the pain, but it'll settle now. In a little while, if it's OK with you, Jonas will bring the kids in. They'll want to see you.'

'And I want to see them,' Anna whispered. 'Oh, I'm so glad it's over.'

'Aren't we all? Can you ring Dr Lunn in clinic?' Em asked the nurse with her. She glanced at her watch. 'Tell him Anna is back. Tell him I've just given her morphine and she'll sleep for an hour or so, but after that…if he could bring in the kids, I'll take over clinic.'

And that was that.

She didn't see Jonas for the rest of the day, and if that was deliberate on Em's part then who could blame her? She desperately needed time out. She was so confused she was having trouble concentrating on medicine.

And when she returned to the house that night, Robby was alone with Amy. Jonas was still out with the kids.

Maybe he needed time out, too, she thought, and if there was a trace of bitterness in her thoughts, who could blame her for that either? The man had stirred up so much unwanted emotion within her. It was to be hoped he felt a little bit stirred up as well!

She played with Robby for a while, then settled him to sleep. Then she left him in the care of the night staff and went through to the hospital to do a late round. She was expecting Anna to be alone. Instead, she found her with Jonas.

And her blasted emotions were stirred all over again.

'What have you done with the kids?' she asked. She raised her eyebrows at Jonas, and then smiled down at Anna in mock indignation. 'He's a fine babysitter, I don't think.'

But Jonas was indignant in his turn. 'I haven't abandoned them. Jim's taken them out for pizza.'

'Jim?' Em's eyebrows rose still further. 'Jim Bainbridge?'

To her surprise—and delight—a faint trace of colour was sweeping over Anna's pale face. Well, well. So it wasn't all one way.

'He offered,' she said defensively. 'And the kids know him. He just lives over the back fence. He...' Her colour mounted still further. 'He came up to Blairglen but I didn't want to see him. Then he waited for a couple of hours to see me here. In the end, I had to say I'd see him. And he wanted to do something so much.'

'I think it's a fine idea,' Em said soundly. She picked up Anna's observation chart to do a quick check and smiled down again at her patient. 'Sometimes it takes courage to accept that people want desperately to help. I think, often, it's easier to be the giver than the receiver.'

Anna nodded. 'I'm not used...to receiving.'

'Now, how did I guess that?' Another smile, this time including Jonas. 'These obs are good. The trip here doesn't seem to have upset you too much. Everything's looking fine, Anna. Now I'll leave you with your brother,' Em said gently, but Anna shook her head.

'I'd like Jonas to leave, too,' she said. 'Please... I want to be alone.'

'She always wants to be alone.'

Back in their shared living room, Jonas was pacing like a caged tiger, his frustration showing. 'Hell. How can I let her see how much I want to be near?'

Em watched him pace. Robby had just woken and she was cuddling him. The baby was crooning his happiness to be reunited with her and she was undergoing all sorts of pain herself—but she felt for Jonas.

And she also felt for Anna.

'Your parents hurt her badly,' she said softly. 'As they hurt you. She's learned the hard way to be independent.'

'If I was in this situation—'

'Would you depend on other people?' She looked at him thoughtfully. 'I don't think so.'

'Of course I would.'

'Emotionally?' She rose and hugged Robby tighter. The baby snuggled against her breast, and Em's heart twisted. 'I'm not sure whether you know the meaning of the words emotional dependency.' She certainly did.

But Jonas was turning on her, confused. 'I don't know what you're trying to say.'

'Of course you don't.' She took a deep breath, trying to figure the best way to say it. 'Jonas, do you need Anna?'

He stared at her blankly. 'She's my little sister.'

'I know that. But do you need her? Have you ever shown her that?'

'I don't need her,' he said, his voice still uncomprehending. 'Of course I don't. I've always been the strong one.'

'Because you've had to be. But emotional dependency works both ways.' She took a deep breath and looked down at Robby. 'Take me and Robby.'

'Now, that's another thing—'

'Robby needs me,' she said, ignoring the interruption. 'At least, he needs someone to love him to bits. Which I could do so easily. But I have the honesty to acknowledge that I need Robby, too.'

'You don't need Robby. He's a baby.'

'But he gives.' Em looked down at the child in her arms

and her face changed. 'Every time he grins at me, every time I have to hurt him when I change his dressings or massage his little limbs, and he doesn't cry because he knows if I hurt him a cuddle will follow, every time he snuggles into me—that need grows. That's the sort of need I'm talking about. I'm talking about love, Jonas. Anna has learned to survive without it. And I think…so have you.'

'That's ridiculous.'

'No. It's the truth.' A knock sounded through the house and she sighed and put her emotions on the back-burner. 'This'll be Jim, bringing the children home. He's another one like me. Who loves—and needs—and who doesn't stand a donkey's chance of being loved and needed in return.'

Jonas stared at her blankly, not having the faintest clue what she was talking about. He was so blind! 'You're over-dramatising.'

But as Em went to answer the door she knew she wasn't.

She loved and needed. And she was desperate to be loved and needed in return.

And it wasn't just the little boy in her arms who was engendering these dangerous emotions.

It was Jonas Lunn!

CHAPTER EIGHT

THE days after Anna's operation became a week. And then two.

Work and domesticity settled into a pattern Em found almost acceptable—if only her stupid emotions didn't get in the way.

Once Anna's drainage tube came out, she was allowed home. Her children went with her. She refused to let Jonas stay with her—he stayed on with Em, whether Em thought it was wise or not—but Anna *did* allow her brother to organise home help.

That was something, at least, Em thought. The prickly Anna of old wouldn't even have allowed that.

And as for Jonas...

Jonas was frustrated with the little help he could give his sister. There was so little he could do!

He did insist on spending time each day with Ruby and Sam and Matt, using his wish to establish bonds with them as a way to give Anna much needed child care. He also threw himself into working for the town. He did what he could.

For both the women he was helping...

At least Em was a skilled doctor, he thought as he worked on beside her. He could trust her to look after Anna. And at least, with him staying on as her temporary partner, she had time to do it properly. Do house calls. Care...

She would have done it anyway, he knew, but in the

equation without him, there would have been no time at all for Robby, or for Em herself.

She would have worked herself into a breakdown.

It wasn't that she was driven to work, he decided, although he knew doctors who were consumed with their jobs. Em wasn't like that. She simply found it impossible to reject pleas for help. She never said no, and it made no difference how tired she was, or how long the queue waiting in the surgery.

So he'd saved her from that—temporarily—but the more he saw of her—the more he saw of her medicine and her caring—the more he wondered how he could possibly leave at the end of Anna's radiotherapy.

An idea was starting to stir and shift at the back of his mind...

Physically, Anna was recovering brilliantly, though neither Jonas nor Em were so sure about emotionally.

Anna read all the literature, and then deliberately left it behind in the hospital. Well over ninety percent survival, the books said, which backed up what the doctors had told her. She could live with that. Sure, the oncologist had said her chances would be even better if she had chemotherapy, but that meant months of depending on others for help, and she rejected it out of hand.

So live she did, but on her own terms. She went about organising the radiotherapy but, despite Jonas's offer to rent an apartment in Blairglen for them all, she made the decision to travel to Blairglen every day.

'So I can still be independent. Lori will look after the kids during the day and I can still be with them at night.'

And Lori, due to return to Bay Beach any day, was willing to take them on.

'It's not the easiest solution for you,' Em told Anna. 'The travelling will make you tired.'

But Anna wasn't giving in. 'I don't want to be any more dependent on Jonas than I already am,' Anna said definitely, and Em could only watch as his sister drove Jonas as far away as she could.

And Anna was also driving Jim away.

The fire chief came to see Em in surgery, ostensibly for a twisted little finger but in truth to tell her how concerned he was about Anna.

'She won't let me help,' he told her sadly. 'She won't let me near.'

Em could only shake her head. There was no advice she could give. If she had any way of breaking down barriers, she'd be breaking them down herself.

The time she'd spent with Jonas and four children seemed now like an amazing dream. That sensation of family had eased now that Anna's three children had left. With Amy's help, Em could look after Robby without Jonas's assistance, and Jonas seemed to want that. So there was less and less need for Jonas and her to be together.

But separation hurt. Em was hurting. Even her dog was pining. Bernard was back to his old, lethargic self.

And here was Jim, and he was hurting, too.

'Do you really want me to do anything about this finger?' Em asked the fire chief, examining the offending digit. 'I could refer you to an orthopaedic surgeon for resetting, but it looks like it was broken years ago. Is it causing any trouble?'

'Yeah, well, it *was* broken years ago and, no, it's not causing trouble,' he admitted. 'I sort of wanted an excuse to talk to you.'

'Now, why did I suspect that?'

'Are you getting on any better with her brother than I am with Anna?'

Em frowned, and spent some more time unnecessarily examining his finger. Getting her face in order. 'I don't know what you mean.'

'I mean there's two Lunns,' Jim said grimly. 'There's two people who are fighting shy of attachment. At least you have yours living with you. Working side by side...'

And a fat lot of good that was doing her, Em thought bleakly.

It might halve her workload, but in every other respect it was just making life impossible.

Lori returned to Bay Beach the following day, cheerful, optimistic and ready to return to being a home mother.

'Ray's out of danger. His operation went really, really well,' she told Em and Jonas. 'All he needs is a whole heap of advice from the dietician and he'll be back at work. Like I will be tomorrow.'

'We've missed you.' It was Jonas. They'd just finished dinner, and Em was giving Robby his last bottle for the night. She'd been standing at the window, rocking him to sleep, when Lori had dropped in to see them all.

We've missed you...

Em flashed Jonas a quick look and couldn't quite keep the resentment out of her tone when she added, 'Yeah. Jonas has had to do some babysitting.'

'I've done it really well,' he said indignantly, and Lori smiled. Her smile was only surface deep, though. Suddenly her active mind was working overtime. There were undercurrents here that she couldn't read.

'Do you want me to take Robby home with me tonight?' she asked, and Em almost gasped. Instead, she took a deep, steadying breath.

This had to happen some time, she told herself, trying hard not to look down at the baby in her arms. Well, why not? It was logical. Lori was Robby's carer. Not her.

'Maybe it'd be for the best,' she said, but her voice didn't sound like hers at all.

'The best for whom?' Jonas asked indifferently, and Em could have slapped him.

'For Robby, of course,' she snapped.

'You're only thinking of Robby?'

'Who else would I be thinking of?'

'Yourself,' Jonas said mildly, and watched her face.

'Why…why…?'

'Because you love the kid,' Jonas told her, as if she were a little bit stupid, and as if he didn't see what the problem was. 'I don't see why you don't adopt him yourself. Heck, anyone can see you think the sun rises and sets with him.'

'And you think that'd be OK,' Em snapped. 'I've been able to spend heaps of time with him these last couple of weeks, but that's only because you've been here to help with my workload. As soon as you go, I'll have to depend totally on Amy—a teenager who'll take off with her own life any minute. That's no basis for adoption. Me being a mother for short bursts at night? I don't think so!'

'You'd be a mother who loves her baby, though,' Jonas said thoughtfully. 'That's more than a lot of kids have.'

'It wouldn't work.' Lori's quick eyes had been assessing the pair of them. She was as concerned as Em as to Robby's fate, and she was very, very interested in these undercurrents. 'For a start, Tom wouldn't allow it.'

'Tom?' Jonas's eyebrows snapped a question.

'Our director.' Lori shook her head when she thought about him. 'There's an assessment committee, but the final decision comes down to Tom. He decides whether a couple—or a single person—would make good parents, and he's very good at his job.'

'You're saying Em wouldn't make a good mother?'

'I'm saying Em wouldn't stand a chance of being permitted to adopt,' Lori said bluntly. 'An overworked single mum… Tom would say that she'd never hack the pace.'

'So he'd discriminate because she's single.'

'No. If she was working half-time she'd get a look-in—a good look-in because Tom would soon figure out how much she cares. But our Em works eighty-hour weeks or more. He'd discriminate, and rightly so because she doesn't have time.'

'But if she was married…' Jonas said thoughtfully, and let the room fade to silence. 'Would that make a difference?'

'Of course it would,' Lori told him, after a moment's stunned silence. She frowned and very carefully didn't look at Em. She concentrated on Jonas. They were all standing—Jonas from when he'd answered the door and Em still at her watching place by the window. Only she wasn't watching the window. 'Is it likely?' Lori asked at last. 'That our Em could be married?'

'I suppose it could be,' Jonas told her, as if the idea had only just occurred to him.

'How could it be?' Lori asked bluntly.

'She could be married to me.'

For a moment there was absolute silence. Not even the clock ticked. The world held its breath, waiting for the bomb Jonas had just lobbed to explode into a million fragments and destroy everything around it.

Maybe it already had. For when Em's breathing returned to a semblance of normality, her world had tilted on its axis, so much so that she felt like she was about to fall off.

What had he said?

'I beg your pardon?' Lori said, and Em could only cast her a grateful glance. For herself, she was totally unable to speak.

'I mean Em and I could get married,' Jonas said mildly. 'It's been done before. Marriages of convenience.'

'Yes, but—'

'Look, it's simple,' he said reasonably. 'I'm not the least bit interested in marriage. I never have been. And Em doesn't want—hasn't time for—a proper husband. However, she wants Robby.' He smiled, his gorgeous, crooked smile that did so much damage to Em's heart. 'I can see what the problem is, and I'm sure you can, too, Lori. I haven't been staying with Em for this long without realising she's tearing her heart out to keep Robby. And this way she could.'

'How could she?' Lori sounded fascinated.

Em, on the other hand, was just plain dumbfounded. She had to find a chair and sit. So she sat and held onto Robby like she was drowning, gazing up at Jonas in stupefaction.

'Easy.'

'It's not easy.' Lori had been under a fair amount of strain over the past couple of weeks and her normal placid self wasn't what it should have been. She let an edge of annoyance show. 'You're a city surgeon. I assume you don't want to practise here, in Bay Beach.'

'No. Well, not totally, but…'

'But what?' Lori glared. She cast an uncertain glance at Em, then went right on glaring. She was starting to think this man was an insensitive oaf. The way Em looked… She looked like her world was crumbling.

She looked like she loved this man, Lori thought suddenly. She was watching Jonas as if he was close to the most precious thing in the world, rating as precious as the child she held in her arms.

And Jonas was talking as if the whole thing was a business proposition.

'Tom's going to want to know who's intending to look after Robby,' Lori snapped. 'You're not offering to be Robby's daddy?'

'No.' But Jonas's voice was suddenly uncertain. 'Except…sometimes.'

'This is crazy.' Em interrupted them both from where she sat. 'Just crazy! Lori, go home. The man's talking nonsense.'

'I'm not talking nonsense.' Jonas's voice firmed. 'It could work.'

'How could it work?' Em's voice was a desperate whisper, and Jonas gave a wry smile.

'Hey, Em, there's no need to get your knickers in a twist. I'm not offering human sacrifice here. I'm offering a business proposition.'

'Which is?'

'I've been thinking,' he said, and for the first time a trace of uncertainty entered his voice. Like he was a little unsure himself why he was doing what he was doing. But he *had* been thinking things through. It did make sense. Sort of. 'You know I was offered a teaching job overseas before I came here?'

'Yes.'

Em cast an uncertain glance at Lori, but Lori was riveted. She was listening to a proposal of marriage. Lori should get herself out of here and leave them to it, but she didn't look like she intended moving for quids!

And Jonas kept right on speaking. 'I really want at least a part-time teaching job,' he told Em, and he was ignoring Lori now, speaking directly to her. To his intended…*wife*?

'I enjoy teaching,' he told her. 'I've been doing some in Sydney but there's not enough for a full-time position. For the rest of the time I've been doing increasingly technical surgery, which I haven't been enjoying much at all.'

'I don't—'

But he wasn't brooking interruptions, and he was still focusing on Em. Trying to make her see.

'Em, increasingly, my area of expertise is patient-surgeon interaction. In fact, I've written papers and presented theories on healing times improving with better communication.' He gave a self-conscious grin. 'And they do. I've been working through guidelines for surgeons to discuss with their patients before and after surgery, including such things as fear of outcome, fear of pain—even such things as family problems. Things many surgeons don't think they have time for. That's my soapbox, really, and it's what's important to me. The surgery itself, although important, is no longer my chief priority.'

'I don't see what this has to do with me.' This was hard. Em could hardly find the strength to speak. What had he said? *Marriage!* She was rocking Robby back and forth, clutching him like a lifeline, and Lori was looking from Jonas to Em and back again with the alertness of a particularly interested sparrow.

'Simply this.' Jonas sighed. 'I've been at a crossroads. I don't want to work myself into the ground to become the world's greatest vascular or any other specialist surgeon. But I'm being pushed that way in Sydney, and it's taking all my time to keep up with the current technologies. That was why I accepted the teaching job overseas but, to be honest, I was still unsure about that. I thought, even though I didn't want to be a specialist surgeon, I'd miss surgery—medicine—itself. Hands-on patient work. So I'd sort of like...' He cast a quick glance at Em before he kept on speaking. 'I'd sort of like to return to general surgery in the real sense. With maybe a bit of general practice on the side.'

'You mean you *do* want to practise in Bay Beach,' Lori breathed, and Em sent her a helpless glance. Good grief! She had an almost irresistible urge to drum her heels on the door and yell.

But she couldn't. Jonas was still speaking.

'I talked to Chris Maitland, the doctor who works south of here,' he told her. 'Did you know he's a specialist anaesthetist?'

Em did. 'Yes, but—'

'He did the same as me,' Jonas told her. 'He became fed up with the lack of human contact in big city medicine, so he went back to general practice. But if I came here I wouldn't have to give up surgery entirely, and Chris could resurrect his anaesthetics. I could do all the surgery for the district—we'd hardly have to use Blairglen—plus I could do a bit of general practice on the side. I could keep up my research and one or two days a week I could travel to Sydney and do my teaching.'

He frowned and he was looking inward, still thinking it through. Seeing possibilities...

'And if I'm teaching through the training hospitals, I reckon I could get teaching status for this district. If we had interns on rotation, how much easier would that make life for everyone?'

How much easier?

It made Em's mind go blank just to try to take it in. Jonas here, and first-year doctors rotating to do part of their training here as well...

Bliss!

But that wasn't what they were talking about. They were talking about marriage.

'I don't—'

'Hey, I'm leaving.' Em had almost forgotten Lori's presence, but now her friend leaned down and gave her a swift hug, including Robby in her embrace. 'This is getting far too complicated for me. All I know is that you don't want to give Robby up tonight.' And she smiled warmly down into her friend's eyes, sending her a silent message. 'And you might not want to give him up—ever.'

'Lori—'

'Don't be too hasty,' Lori told her. 'Listen to what the man has to say. And think about what you could get out of this.'

'I wouldn't—'

'You might,' Lori told her firmly. 'I'm going. You just listen!'

Silence.

The silence went on and on and on. The echo of the door slamming after Lori seemed to reverberate for minutes, while Em sat and hugged Robby and tried to come to terms with what Jonas had just offered.

It still didn't make any sense.

'You want to stay here,' she said at last. 'Is that what it is?'

'I want a base,' he told her. 'I've decided that. I like your kind of medicine. I've fallen for Anna's kids in a big way. I see that her need of family will be ongoing, and this way—'

'You could just work here,' she said desperately. 'Heavens, we need you enough. There's no need for this ridiculous talk of marriage.'

'No.' His eyes turned thoughtful. 'I didn't think so either. But then there's Robby. If I marry you, Robby will have a family.'

'You don't want to be Robby's father. You just said so.'

'I did,' he admitted. 'I don't want to be anyone's father.' And then his voice changed.

He was watching Robby. Robby was very close to sleep. He'd been lying contentedly in Em's arms, looking out at this bright wondrous world around him. Now he was snuggling close, his tiny lashes were fluttering closed and his little fist closed around Em's fingers.

He was so damaged! The elastic bandages on his arm looked stark and white, real evidence of what was before him.

'I don't want him to stay in an orphanage,' he said, and his voice was still changed—husky with emotion, and strained—as if he couldn't believe what he was feeling, and he was fighting it every inch of the way.

'You've fallen for him, too,' Em said, watching his face, and he gave a reluctant nod.

'Yes. I guess I have. He's a brave little kid. So if by marrying you I could get him a home...'

'That's some sacrifice!'

He smiled at that, a wry, half-mocking smile. 'Hey, you're not that bad.'

But I'm not that good, Em thought desperately, and waited.

'Would we live together?' she asked curiously.

He raked his hair and thought about that for a bit. 'I guess we'd need to if we were to formally adopt Robby, but I can't see it as a problem. I'd be in Sydney a bit, and this house is plenty big enough for all of us. And if we had a trainee doctor living here as well, it wouldn't get too personal.'

Not too personal!

Personal! A fate worse than death, obviously!

'But this would be a long-term thing,' Em said wildly. 'You'd have to tell Tom you'd be prepared to be Robby's father. If we...*we*, Jonas. Not me. If *we* were to adopt him then you'd need to be involved.'

'I don't see that. Not if he has you.'

She took a deep breath, fighting back the emotions surging around her so fast she felt her head was about to spin off her shoulders. 'Jonas, I want Robby so badly it hurts,' she told him. 'But Robby needs a family.'

She closed her eyes, trying desperately to stay calm. To think clearly. Because what Jonas was offering was almost unbelievably tempting.

But she knew she couldn't take it.

She had one small problem. And she had to tell him. The only way forward here was honestly, no matter how much pride was at stake.

'Jonas, I think you should know that I've fallen in love with you,' she said bluntly, and her eyes didn't leave his face. 'I think you should factor that into any equation you make. You see, I don't think I could live in the same house as you—as your wife—and stay...impersonal.'

His face froze. He stared at her like she'd just uttered an obscenity.

'You *what*?'

But the time for prevarication was over. There was only room for the truth.

'I've fallen for you in a big way, Jonas Lunn,' she told him, tilting her chin and meeting his look head on. With dignity and with courage. 'So if you're asking me to marry you—for keeps—then I'd say thank you very much, I'd love to, because I'd like nothing better than to be your wife. But I would be your *wife*, Jonas. In every sense of the word.'

'Em!' He was clearly flabbergasted.

'Stupid, isn't it?' she said cordially. 'Unprofessional. Self-destructive even. For me and for Robby. Because if I didn't…love you…maybe I could accept what you're offering.'

'What I'm offering makes sense,' he said explosively. 'Whereas what you're saying…'

'Doesn't make sense at all,' she agreed.

'So forget you said it. You don't mean it.'

She closed her eyes again. How could he be so blind?

'I do mean it,' she said at last. 'I mean it more than anything I've ever said in my life. I didn't mean to fall in love. I never intended it. It just sort of happened. So…so it wouldn't work. Having half the cake but not the half I want most. I'd have a child and a husband— but a husband who treats me as a professional colleague.'

'What more do you want, for heaven's sake? How can you need more?' He sounded angry, and suddenly so was she. He was so damned insensitive. So…

So Jonas.

'I want it all,' she told him simply, and her chin was still tilted at that dangerous angle that said she was taking on the world. Or she was giving it up. 'I knew when I came here that my chances of having a husband and children were about nil. I accepted that. But now you're offering half of what I want most in life, and I find…I find that I'd rather not have anything at all than constantly living—seeing—the other half. The half that's out of my reach.'

Silence.

He looked baffled, she thought. He so totally didn't understand.

'You want Robby,' he said.

'I do.' She was close to tears. 'But you don't want us.' She bit her lip. 'Oh, sure, you say you don't want Robby

to have to stay in an orphanage. So you'll sacrifice yourself for us. Marry me. But I'm not prepared to carry that
load of sacrifice. Not marriage, Jonas. Not…not without
love.'

'We don't…love,' he said slowly. His anger was fading
as he saw the distress on her face. 'Not my sister and I.
We can't. Em, I'm sorry, but we've had love knocked out
of us from an early age.'

'And you can't get it back?'

'I don't want to,' he said honestly. 'It hurts too damned
much.'

'It takes courage.'

'No. It takes courage to be independent. If you knew
how much I wanted…' He caught himself, and almost
perceptibly drew back. 'No! I'm sorry, Em, but that's the
offer.'

'And is it all or nothing?' she said bleakly. 'Either I
marry you on your terms or you'll ride off into the sunset
without a backward glance?'

He glanced down at Robby. 'I don't know. I'll have to
think about it. You really won't marry me?'

There was only the one answer possible. 'No.'

'I still need a base.'

'Not with me.'

He thought about that, and then slowly nodded, read-
justing his thinking. 'OK. OK, I'll accept that. I think it's
stupid, but maybe if I stayed anyway we could work
things out. If I told Anna I was staying here so you could
adopt Robby, she'd accept that. She wouldn't think I was
just doing it for her.'

'Are you doing it just for her?' Em asked curiously,
and then watched Jonas's face change. He didn't know
himself, she thought. He was trying so darn hard to be
independent, but he wasn't independent at all.

He'd told himself he was making this offer for Anna, but a part of him wanted Robby—and a part of him wanted the sense of community he'd found in Bay Beach.

If only a part of him wanted her...

But he wasn't admitting to that! Concentrate on Robby.

He was thinking that, too. He could persuade her by thinking of Robby. 'You might still be able to adopt Robby, if I was here to help,' he told her, thinking it through as he spoke. 'If I could arrange the medical needs of the community so you had free time, then Tom might be swayed to let you keep him.'

He might. That was something at least. Em's heart gave a tiny lift, but she looked across at Jonas and the spurt of joy faded. Jonas was so near. So close.

And she had to drive him away.

'It'd be so much easier if you married me,' he said, and waited.

This was her second chance.

But she couldn't do it. Not for Robby.

And not for herself. Marriage without love was the way of madness.

'No, Jonas, it'd be much harder,' she told him gently. 'For all of us.'

CHAPTER NINE

'YOU are out of your mind!'

'Sorry?'

'You have turned down Jonas Lunn? Emily Mainwaring, you are nutty about the man. I have eyes in my head. You're head over heels in love with him and you've turned down a proposal of marriage!'

Lori's voice rose so high it was practically a squeak.

She plonked herself down on the chair beside Em's desk and gazed at her friend in stupefaction.

'All our problems would be solved,' she said bleakly. 'We'd have a new doctor for Bay Beach. We'd have parents for Robby. End of loneliness for you. Plus a sex life. And you turn the man down!'

'He didn't mention a sex life.' Em said very carefully, staring at her prescription pad rather than at her friend.

That set Lori back.

'You mean...'

'I mean, after you left we stayed in exactly the same positions—him on one side of the room and me on the other—while we talked technicalities about how a marriage would work. He thought it was a really sensible business proposition. In fact...' She took a deep breath. 'In fact, I think he might even let himself get fond of Robby. But from a distance.

'He's not that tough,' Lori said weakly, but Em bit her lip.

'He is. He's been taught the hard way how to be impersonal—tough, as you say—and he's not about to un-learn it. Just because…'

'Just because you love him?'

'Just because I love him.' Em raised her face and met Lori's concerned gaze. 'That's it in a nutshell, Lori. I love the guy.'

'And it'd drive you crazy to be married to him when he doesn't love you.'

'You do understand,' Em said gratefully. 'If Ray didn't love you…'

'I'd go quietly insane,' Lori told her. 'I didn't realise until I nearly lost him. That's one of the reasons I'm here. We're getting married in a month's time and I want you as my maid of honour. Will you do it?'

'Of course I will.'

'But there's no chance of you marrying first? Of you being my matron of honour?'

'Lori, I can't.'

Lori looked at her friend over her surgery desk and knew that Em spoke the absolute truth.

And she also knew that her friend was breaking her heart.

'I don't want him adopted by a single mother.'

It was Robby's aunt. She was facing Tom and Em in Em's surgery, and she was angry. 'What'll people think? That I let my sister's kid be adopted by a single mum when I should take care of him myself?'

Tom's hands clenched on his knees. Em could see them from where she sat. As the director of the children's homes, Tom was accustomed to all sorts of family dramas, but he still had the ability to be emotionally involved. And who could help being moved by Robby's situation?

'Laura, you're saying you don't want him, but you also

demand that he must stay in Bay Beach and he must be adopted by a married couple?'

'That's right.'

'But he's badly scarred,' Tom said gently. 'There's ongoing injury. You know that. Robby has years and years of skin grafts ahead of him. He needs constant medical attention. Em wants to give him just that—and a mother's love as well. I don't think you'll find anyone else to take him on. Not with his injuries.'

'Then he stays in the children's home,' Laura said obstinately. 'You're not blackmailing me into anything else. I know what my sister would want if she was alive to tell me.'

'Surely she'd just want someone to love Robby.'

'But she wouldn't want the community to say I'd shoved my sister's kid off onto a single mum. Dr Mainwaring can look after him short term if she likes,' she added diffidently. 'I can say it's a short-term arrangement until he's better and people will see that it's sensible. In fact, I don't care who does the short-term caring as long as he's treated properly. But no adoption. Unless she's married. No way!'

'That short term is likely to become long term,' Tom warned. 'Which is unsatisfactory for everybody. Robby needs permanence.'

'Then find him a family. Here. A family who'll accept him, injuries and all.'

And that was that.

Em went back to Robby that night, cuddled him to sleep and thought about what she was doing. No adoption...

It meant she could care for Robby for now, but he could be taken from her at any time.

It couldn't matter. She was all he had, for now.

Bernard was lying at her feet. Amazingly, the big dog lifted his head and stirred his tail, looking up at her with soulful eyes that told her he was missing the noise and excitement of Anna's kids, and he didn't understand where they'd gone.

And in the next room Em could hear Jonas moving around, getting ready for bed.

'We have all the pieces of a jigsaw-puzzle,' Em told her ancient dog. 'What we need now is a miracle-worker to put them together. And somehow I don't think that's going to happen. Miracle-workers are a bit thin on the ground around here.'

Next door Jonas was telling himself he needed no such thing as a miracle. What more did they need than the elements they had right now?

Em was being pig-headed, he told himself. His vision of their marriage could work for all of them. If only she could forget this stupid need for emotional involvement.

He couldn't give what he'd never been taught, he thought. He couldn't give what scared him to admit even existed.

But what was happening now was ridiculous. Holding each other at arm's length—not being permitted to adopt Robby—it was silly. It was crazy, and it was all because Em had this damned fool idea that she was in love with him.

It was *stupid*!

And he couldn't go down her road, he told himself over and over. He couldn't. He wanted this family—he wanted to hold it together and marriage would be the binder—but Em wanted more.

She thought love had to be present to hold them.

Love...

He *was* prepared to love, he thought—in an abstract sort of way. He just...

He just couldn't let himself need.

'You're a coward, Lunn,' he said into the darkness—and he knew that he was right.

But there was nothing he could do about it.

Nothing at all.

The medical set-up of Bay Beach was transformed almost overnight. Once set on a course of action, Jonas was determined to see it through, and he almost seemed like a man driven.

OK, Em wouldn't agree to marrying him, but she sure as heck needed him to stay—as did Anna—and he wouldn't let them down for want of trying.

So schedules were made up. Surgery equipment ordered. Lou was employed full time to cope with two doctors instead of one, and Amy was given a permanent part-time job as babysitter.

Jonas moved right into the medical scene of Bay Beach as if he was in charge.

Which made Em feel really, really strange.

She should feel resentful that he seemed to be taking charge, she told herself. She should feel as if she was being made redundant.

In truth, she didn't have a clue how she was supposed to feel. Jonas was one fine surgeon, he wanted to work here and she couldn't stop him. That'd be crazy.

And to marry him would be crazier still.

Her world was spinning out of control. If Jonas seemed in charge it was just as well, she told herself desperately, because nobody else was!

Anna continued to improve. Em took to popping in on her every couple of days, just to see how she was managing and to check her arm. She was coping fine physically, but Em still wasn't sure how Anna was mentally.

'Radiotherapy starts next week,' Em reminded Anna. 'Unless you change your mind and have chemotherapy as well.'

'I won't.'

'You know, even though the benefit for you is slight, I wish you wouldn't completely dismiss it out of hand,' Em said mildly. 'The chances of recurrence now is really small, but with the added insurance of chemotherapy it'd be tiny. Why do I get the feeling you won't even consider it—just because it'd make you more dependent on people in the short term?'

Anna flushed. Em had hit the nail on the head and she knew it.

'I hate it,' she admitted. 'I hate it that I can't hang up my washing. I hate it that I can't lift Ruby...'

'That'll pass. Once your arm settles, you'll be just as strong as you were before. Lymphoedema's becoming more and more rare as surgical techniques improve, and Patrick's a great surgeon. I'd be amazed if there's any long-term problems at all.'

'But I have short-term problems,' Anna threw at her. 'That's enough. I hate being dependent at all, and chemotherapy would make things worse. I hate it that everyone worries. I hate it that Jonas is still here—watching me. I hate it that Jim calls in every night...'

'Anna, they love you.'

'And I don't know what love is, and I don't want to.' She shook her head. 'Neither does Jonas,' she added bitterly. 'The only reason he's here is that I'm his kid sister. I'm something he has to care for because it's his duty. Plus he's staying on because he has this thing going with you that I don't understand. But I'll bet it's not love as normal people know it. Is it?'

Em caught her breath, unable to think of what on earth to say in reply, but it seemed an answer wasn't wanted. Anna hadn't finished. 'Whatever it is, it's just silly that he's staying,' she told Em. 'But he won't budge. And as for Jim... Did you know he asked me to marry him? *Marriage? Me.* A woman with three kids and half a breast. If he thinks I'm such a charity case...'

'I'm sure Jim's not doing it because he feels sorry for you,' Em said quickly, and she knew she was right.

'So you think I should marry him?'

'That's your business.' Em took a deep breath. 'But you'd have to love him.'

'Like you love my brother?'

That set her back. 'What do you mean?'

'I mean Jonas said he wants to marry you. He said that's the main reason he's sticking around. Because of you.'

'I think you'll find it's because of you.'

'Because of me. That's a laugh.' Anna shook her head. 'No one cares that much for me, and no one's going to.'

'They would if you let them.'

'No way.' She shook her head. 'Me and Jonas,' she said bitterly. 'We've seen what love can do. It destroyed my parents and it nearly destroyed us. And that's my last word. I can't believe Jonas wants to marry you, but if he does then you're sensible for refusing him. Because he's just as emotionally damaged as I am.'

And that was that. Em worked on in a fog of uncertainty and misery.

Sure, she had her Robby. Jonas's presence meant that at least she could keep caring for her precious baby. Jonas did morning surgery now, which meant that Em woke to a morning free to spend with her beloved Robby. Which was blissful.

They started taking long walks, and even the somnolent Bernard began reluctantly to enjoy them, loping along beside the pram like a walking doormat. And all the time Em thought and thought. And thought some more.

She was being stupid, she told herself. She was pining for something that didn't exist.

Jonas's love. Ha!

But while Em looked increasingly haggard, Robby bloomed. His scarred little body began to heal faster than Em had anticipated, and she fell for him harder and harder by the day.

Talk to herself as she might, and chastise herself over and over again, it made no difference. She also fell harder and harder for Jonas.

He was always *there*, she thought desperately. Just there. He was either knocking on her door to check on a question about a patient, or asking her to do a minor anaesthetic for him, or finding out the background of a tricky patient. Or he'd be in the ward as she did her hospital rounds...

Or he'd be in her sitting room reading the paper, or working on his referrals or medico-legal stuff, or taking his turn cooking the dinner...

And even if he wasn't physically present, he was in her thoughts.

They had to find some alternative living arrangement, Em decided desperately, a few days before Anna started her radiotherapy. She decided that even though she loved him living in her house. She loved it that Jonas was in her life—that he brought his niece and nephews around to cheer up Bernard and play with Robby...

She loved every part of it.

But it was breaking her apart.

'There's a fisherman's cottage coming up for lease at the end of the month,' she told him. He was cooking them a stir-fry, a silly, frilly apron of Em's protecting his casual trousers and open-necked shirt. It didn't make him look one whit less masculine. In fact, he looked impossibly handsome.

Bernard was lying adoringly at his feet, waiting for him to drop something, and Robby was waving his toes in the air in his carrycot—and the sight of so much domesticity was making Em's heart do back flips.

'You want me to look into the lease?' she asked again, and Jonas's hand stilled in his stir-frying.

'Do you want me to leave?'

It had to be said. So she said it. 'Yes. I do. This…this living arrangement can't be long term.'

'Why not?'

'You know why not,' she said desperately. 'How often do I have to spell it out for you, Jonas? You're turning us into a family without the commitment—and I want it all.'

He paused, went back to stirring and then shook his head. 'This works for me,' he said at last. 'I like living with you.'

'Well, I don't like living with you,' she snapped back. 'It's driving me nuts.'

'But I do a great stir-fry.'

He did. It was a major attribute. A man who could cook…

But Em hardened her heart.

'No,' she told him. 'You have to leave. Shall you enquire about the cottage, or shall I?'

'Bernard doesn't want me to go.'

'*I* want you to go.'

He turned then, and looked at her, straight and direct across the room.

'Really, Em? Really?'

'Yes!'

He sighed. Did his shoulders slump just a little? Or was she imagining it?

'OK,' he told her. 'I'll go. If that's what you really want.'

Only it wasn't what she wanted at all! She lay in bed that night and asked herself if she was a fool. To reject marriage, to reject even sharing a house with him...

To reject the chance to stay with him for ever.

'Maybe it'd work,' she whispered into the dark, and her hand crept out to touch Robby's cradle. 'Maybe he'd learn to love us.'

But if he didn't...

It was all just too hard. She turned over and thumped her pillows, and her mind twisted into a million different maybes.

But maybes were too hard!

Maybe Jonas was right. Loving was a big, big mistake.

Em wanted him to go!

Well, he'd expected it, Jonas told himself. After she'd knocked back his marriage proposition, it was the only sensible decision.

She was darned lucky he intended staying on in the town.

No. That was anger speaking, and he forced anger onto the back-burner. OK, he felt anger that she'd turned down what was the most logical plan for all of them. He felt anger that she let her heart get in the way of sense.

But it wasn't sensible for either of them to want Robby,

he thought. And if Em hadn't wanted Robby, would he have wanted this marriage thing so much?

It was all muddled in his mind. Robby. Anna.

Em…

There was a whuffling under his bed, and he put a hand down to discover a large, wet tongue rasping across his hand. Bernard. Well, well. When had Bernard last moved from the comfort of Em's bed?

'You're a dope, dog,' he muttered, thinking of where the dog had come from. 'That's where I'd love to be.'

And then he heard what he'd said.

Was it the truth?

Yes, he acknowledged. Absolutely. Well, why not? Em was the most gorgeous woman he knew. A man would have to be insane not to want to sleep with her.

Or…marry her? That, too.

Just not love her.

'I can't,' he told Bernard a trifle desperately. 'I don't even know how to begin to love someone. And she'd depend on me, and it'd scare me rigid. I'm independent. I've fought all my life to be independent and that's the way I intend to stay.'

Bernard licked again, and Jonas sighed.

'You're telling me I'm not so independent—that I can't walk away and leave everyone. That it's not just Em. It's Anna and her kids. It's Robby. And it's even you, you misbegotten mutt.'

That earned him another slurp and he grinned.

'Hell!'

He was getting deeper and deeper into this quagmire.

'The lady's right. I need at least to get out of here. I need to live alone.'

Only why did the thought seem so bleak?

* * *

Two days to Anna's radiotherapy. Then one.

'Do you want me to come with you the first time?' Jonas asked for what must surely have been the tenth time. 'Anna, it's not something you should face alone.'

'Why? Does it hurt?'

'No. It doesn't hurt at all. It's just a simple X-ray.'

'Well, then…'

'There'll be people there who are sicker than you,' he told her bluntly. 'Proper cancer patients. Not frauds like you.'

That earned him a faint smile, but still Anna shook her head.

'I can cope alone.'

'Some people find it threatening.'

'And so might I,' she admitted. 'But I've never depended on anybody and I don't intend to start now. Jim's already been at me to let him come with me, and I've refused him. So back off, Jonas, and let me be.'

He had no choice but to accept her decision. He was doing a lot of that these days. And the damnable thing was that he knew, in her situation, he'd do exactly the same thing.

So he worked on through the afternoon's list of house calls, he concentrated on his medicine and he knew more and more that he could never depend on anyone. That had been knocked out of him and his sister the hard way.

But Em and Robby needed him. They needed him to stay in the town.

That was all right, he told himself. The need was on Em's side only. Not his.

He didn't need in return.

Ever.

* * *

It was two in the afternoon. Em was at her desk in her surgery and Jonas was out doing a house call on a farmer with gout. This was the Jonas-organised new order. Em was seeing one patient after another, enjoying the sensation that her house calls weren't mounting up as she went. When she finished surgery at six or so, Amy would be waiting to hand over Robby. Then Jonas was on call tonight, so she could get back to being Robby's mother.

Which was lovely.

Or it should have been lovely. There was still this aching need that wouldn't subside, a need that Jonas had created and not filled.

He'd asked her for marriage, but he hadn't needed her. He didn't love…

Medicine!

She needed to concentrate on medicine.

The phone rang. She winced, knowing before she picked up the receiver that it meant an emergency. She was in the middle of Erica Harris's litany of complaints and Lou didn't interrupt a consultation by putting a call through unless it was absolutely vital.

And it was. The normally unflappable Lou sounded shocked and sick.

'Em, it's Anna Lunn's little boy, Sam.'

Em's heart sank. The voice Lou was using spelt disaster.

'What is it?'

'Anna has just rung, and she's almost hysterical. It seems Sam went up into the bush behind their place—the site of the old gold diggings? Apparently there's an old shaft there that hasn't been filled in. Or she says it looked filled in from the top, but it's collapsed and he's fallen. Anna says she and Matt can hear him calling from about thirty feet down, but they can't get him out. They can't get near him. I'm ringing the emergency services but can you go out there, too?'

Of course. She'd already left. Erica Harris was left sitting with her mouth open.

'Find Jonas,' Em snapped at Lou as she flew past. 'Explain to Mrs Harris.'

And she was gone.

CHAPTER TEN

THE mineshaft was about half a mile from Anna's house, back in the hills merging into the national park. Gold had been found here a hundred years ago and mine after mine had been sunk, but gradually most of them had been filled in. Some of the bigger ones had been professionally capped, but this one...

Someone had capped it, Anna told them, speaking between sobs of sheer terror, but they'd used only rough timber. Over time the timber had become covered with bush litter, the wood had rotted and Sam had stepped on the wrong spot and plunged down.

'And I never would have found him if Matt hadn't been with him and come to get me.' Anna subsided into tears on Em's shoulder, and Em held her tightly. Willing her strength...

As well as the terror she was facing, Anna was close to exhaustion, having run to the shaft when Matt had come home screaming for his mother and then run back to the house to telephone Em and Jim. Now she was in the cab of Jim's fire engine, wedged between Em and Jim while the fire chief gunned the truck across the paddocks.

Beside Anna, Jim's face was grim. Like Em, he'd flown to Anna's assistance at the first call. He knew how lethal these mine shafts could be.

'Are you sure he's down there?' The fire chief's voice was curt and filled with concern.

'Matt saw him fall. He raced straight away to find me, and I ran all the way there. He's down there all right. And he's conscious. I've spoken to him. But he sounds so deep. He's fallen so far.' She choked back a sob.

'And I had to leave Matt there,' she whispered as she fought to collect herself. 'I know he's too little to leave while I came for help, but it took us ages to find the hole again and I was scared Sam might stop calling. I couldn't leave Sam alone. If he can't call out there's no way we'd find where the shaft was.'

She broke right down then, and Em's hand came out to take hers. Anna was very close to breaking point anyway. So much had happened to her over the last month.

And now this...

'You did the right thing, Anna,' she told her strongly. 'Now leave the rest to us.'

She had no choice. She'd left Ruby with a neighbour. Once again, Anna had needed to ask for help, but she wasn't holding back. She wanted Em, and she wanted Jim and she wanted anyone else who could help. And especially...

'Jonas,' she whispered. 'Where's Jonas? I need him.'

Now there was an admission!

'Lou's contacting him now,' Em told her. 'He was out doing a house call but he'll meet us there.'

'As soon as we find the shaft, I'll send a man back to bring him through the hills,' Jim said curtly, still concentrating on not overturning the truck. The last thing they wanted was to hit a shaft themselves, but the ground here was clear enough. When they reached the rough country they'd have to get out and walk. Slowly.

'The kids know this isn't safe,' Jim said, and it was as if he was speaking to himself. His voice was grim with foreboding. 'I've told them that, over and over.'

He sounded just like a parent, Em thought. He sounded as frantic as Anna was herself. She looked at the pair of

them, and they looked like partners. If only Anna would
see it.

But she wasn't concentrating on partnerships now.

'I did, too.' Anna took a deep breath. 'But the boys
were mad with me.'

'Why?'

'They overheard Jim asking if he could take them to
the motor show in Blairglen next week,' Anna whispered.
'And they heard me refusing.'

'So they headed for the hills?'

'Sam has a temper,' Anna said, and Jim nodded at that.

'Plus he's as stubborn as a mule,' he told her. 'Just like
his mother.' Then he flicked a glance at Em's white face,
and he nodded again. 'And their uncle,' he added almost
to himself. 'You and Jonas both, Anna Lunn. Of all the
damned fool families for me and Em to fall in love
with…'

He didn't finish. They were at the edge of the cleared
land, and they could go no further in the truck. They piled
out—Anna, Jim and Em, and the six members of the fire
crew from the back of the truck—and Anna led the way
into the bush.

Anna shouldn't be doing this, Em thought worriedly as
the men hacked through the scrub where she indicated.
She was only a few weeks post-op, and if she fell on that
arm, she could do herself real damage.

'Hold Jim's hand, Anna,' she told her. 'With your good
arm. Jim, hold onto her and don't let her fall.'

'I can manage.'

'For heaven's sake, we have one casualty, and I don't
want two,' Em snapped. 'Stop being so darned independent and do what you're told.'

Anna cast her a scared look, Jim gave Em a thumbs-up signal and Anna's hand was taken, whether she liked it or not.

And then they reached Matt.

The little boy was sitting completely by himself on a fallen log. He was one distraught six-year-old, and Em had never seen a child more frightened in her life. There were tears streaming down his face, and he looked as if he'd been crying for ever.

It was all Em could do not to rush forward and gather him into her arms, but Anna was there before her. Despite her still painful arm, she did just that.

'It's OK, sweetheart. We've got help.' Somehow Anna managed to sound coherent. 'Look, Dr Mainwaring's here…and Jim…and all these men. They'll get Sam out.'

But for Matt, it wasn't enough. He'd obviously been speaking to his big brother down the shaft, and he had someone else in mind. 'Sam says we need Uncle Jonas,' he quavered. 'Where's Uncle Jonas?'

'He's right here.'

The voice came out of the bush, and Jonas emerged into the clearing like he'd been conjured.

He must have been right behind them, following the noise they were making as they bush-bashed toward the mine, and how he'd got there so fast, Em didn't know. From where he'd been doing his house call he must have moved like greased lightning. He didn't hold back as Em did, but strode forward and took Anna and Matt into his arms.

And he hugged them both.

Hard.

Then they all stared at the tiny slit in the ground that marked the entrance to the shaft.

Em's heart sank when she saw what was facing them.

The timber covering the shaft was strewn with leaves

and rotten twigs. She could see why neither boy had realised it was a shaft. It was horribly camouflaged. One of the rotten planks under the leaf litter had split, a hole about eighteen inches wide and about two feet long had appeared and Sam had slipped through.

He must have grabbed at the surrounding timber as he'd fallen, because already there were twigs covering the hole. If Matt hadn't been here to see... To guide them back...

It was a miracle that he had. They never would have found this without him.

'Sam?' Jonas released Anna and walked to within four feet of the hole. Here the earth was mounded, tossed out by the miners a hundred years ago so he knew it was solid, but to go any closer would be suicidal.

'Uncle... Uncle Jonas...' It was a sob of pain from way below ground, and Em closed her eyes at the sound. Not only did Sam sound like he was hurt, he also sounded like he was a long, long way down.

Thirty feet, Anna had estimated, and she couldn't be far wrong. Sam's quavery voice echoed into a whisper, sounding over and over through the bush. It was as if he was almost gone from them and only his ghost was lingering.

That was stupid thinking, Em told herself sharply. Get a grip on yourself. The last thing anyone needed here was a hysterical doctor! Or a hysterical anybody. She looked around her, and every single face reflected her terror.

But Jonas had himself under control—sort of—and was answering his nephew.

'We're all here, Sam,' Jonas said strongly back down to him. 'Your mum, Dr Mainwaring, Jim and the men from the fire brigade are all here. And Matt's here, too. He led us to you like a real hero. OK, Sam.' He forced his voice to be matter-of-fact. 'Let's get some action. Can you tell me what you're standing on?'

And the echoing whisper came up. 'I'm not…I'm not standing on anything.'

Not standing on anything… That was the worst possible answer. Em's stomach clenched at the thought of what it meant.

'So what's holding you up?' Jonas said, and Em could detect a faint tremor behind the strength of his words.

Then she glanced back at movement behind her and discovered that the men from the fire brigade were unloading planks from the truck and carrying them toward the shaft. Jim wasn't wasting time.

'My shoulders are stuck,' Sam whimpered. He caught his breath and started again. Every word was obviously a huge effort. 'I fell and fell and then my shoulders wedged against the sides. My feet are waving in air. Uncle Jonas, my arm's really, really hurting but I'm scared to wiggle in case I fall even further.'

'Good boy. Not moving is a really sensible decision.' Somehow Jonas had forced his voice back to normal. 'Are your arms above your head or below?' He said it as if it didn't matter, but everyone knew that it did. Desperately. If his hands were free, maybe someone could be lowered to grasp him and he could be lifted.

But his answer was the wrong one. 'Below. Sort of.' He gave another whimper of pain. 'They're by my sides. One hand's stuck by my tummy, and the other's sort of wedged between my shoulder and the edge. But I can't move anything 'cos there's nothing underneath me. I'm just stuck. Uncle Jonas, I'm scared.'

'As long as you don't move you've no reason to be scared,' Jonas told him, lying without blinking and moving aside for the firemen to lay their planks across from the mound he was standing on to the mound on the other side of the hole. 'Just stay absolutely still, and we'll see what the best way is to get you out of there.'

There wasn't a best way.

Once the men had planks across the entrance, it was Jim who lay on his belly and inched his way across to the crevice. Then he shone his torch downward.

And he said a word that was too low for Sam to hear, but was loud enough for everyone waiting to realise there were huge problems ahead of them.

'There's been land movement here since the shaft was dug,' Jim said briefly as he carefully worked his way back. 'The shaft sides go in and out. The shaft starts off about four foot wide—wide enough for a man to enter with ease. Then about fifteen feet down it narrows to about eighteen inches, before widening again. Sam's dropped further than that.'

'Why?' Jonas was bewildered. 'That doesn't make sense.'

'There was a land tremor here about ten years back,' Jim said briefly. 'A lot of these mines caved in then, but it's my guess this one's just contorted. We'll need to set up mirrors to check for sure, but the shaft seems to narrow again where Sam's stuck. All I can see is Sam's head, and I can tell it's that because I know what I'm looking for. He's so far down... He's stuck firmly by the shoulders—he hasn't even got enough free movement to look up and see the beam of my torch.'

There was silence while this was absorbed. Then Anna gave a racking sob, and Jonas's arm came round her, holding her up. Willing her strength to face what had to be faced.

'We'll get him out, Anna,' he said confidently, then added to Jim, 'Can you get me down there?'

'No way, mate,' Jim told him. 'As I said, the first narrowing's at about fifteen feet. It's too narrow for you to slide through, and if you dislodge any rocks trying then you'll crush Sam.'

'What'll we do?' Anna whispered brokenly. 'Jim... Jonas... Dear God...'

There was no easy answer.

'I want floodlights and mirrors,' Jim said decisively. The fire chief might be emotionally involved but he was still very much in charge. 'We have rods with sights so we can check everything without going down ourselves. The mirrors are designed for looking around corners where we can't. No one goes near that hole until we've had a thorough look at what we're facing.' He took a deep breath. 'Mind you, we still won't be able to tell what depth of shaft Sam has beneath him. Does anyone know how far these shafts drop?'

'My grandpa used to work up in the hills around here,' one of the firemen volunteered. The man was looking as sick as every person there. This was the stuff of nightmares. 'He says there was an old river bed they tried to reach, where the gold lode ran. He's told me...'

'Yes?'

The man's voice had faltered. Now he lifted his head and met Jim's eyes. He deliberately didn't look at Anna. 'He's told me the shafts bottomed at about two hundred feet. That means...if the kid's shoulders slip through from where he's stuck, he has another a hundred and fifty feet to fall. Or more.'

Jim's array of mirrors gave them no comfort at all. It was just as he'd guessed by torchlight—the mine was a shaft about four feet wide, narrowing for a few feet where the land tremor had buckled it, broadening for another ten feet or so and narrowing again where Sam was wedged. They could only imagine the drop underneath.

'There's only one thing to do,' Jim said at last, and he bit his lip so hard a fleck of blood appeared on the broken skin.

'Which is?' Jonas's voice was hoarse with fear. 'Hell, man, we have to do something.' There was so little they could do when even approaching the shaft meant a fear of rocks falling on the little boy's head.

'There's been cases like this before,' Jim said. He sounded surer than his white face let on. 'I've read about them. It'll take a while but it's proved to be only way. I'll organise the equipment now.'

'To do what?'

'We dig a shaft beside this one,' he told them. 'About ten feet away. Far enough not to dislodge anything in Sam's shaft. We dig down to a few feet below Sam, then we tunnel across, meet his shaft, stick in a false floor and come up underneath him.'

Jonas took a deep breath, while everyone else absorbed this in horror. 'That'll take skilled miners. And days.'

'Not days,' Jim said. 'Not with the amount of help I'll call in. But it may well take until tomorrow. We just have to hope that Sam can keep still for that long.'

'He can't.'

Anna had sunk down onto a fallen log, and she was shaking in fear. 'He's hurting now. He only has to twist…'

'He's a sensible kid.' Jonas was still holding her, but his face was as white as her own.

'He's only eight. And he's hurt.'

They knew she was right. Everyone there knew she was right. The chances of Sam staying still for the long hours this would take were slim to non-existent.

And then Em took a deep breath. How wide had Jim said the narrow part of the shaft was?

'Let me see,' she said. She took Jim's torch before he could protest and crawled across the planking to see for herself. She was very careful, holding the torch clear from the shaft so she could see without dislodging anything.

And she saw exactly what Jim had described. A narrowing fifteen feet down, not wide enough to let a man through, but wide enough to let Sam slip though into the wider chamber beyond and then into the next narrowing.

Not big enough to let a man through…

'Jim, how wide is that blockage at fifteen feet?' she asked in a strained voice. 'Can we find out exactly?'

'I guess.' Jim was watching her from the side of the planking. 'I have instruments in the truck that can do it.'

'Then find out for me,' Em told him. 'If it's wider than my shoulders, I'm going down.'

It took a lot of persuading—about half an hour of constant pressure. There wasn't a man there who wasn't horrified at the thought of *anyone,* much less a woman, going down the shaft.

But there was no choice, and all of them knew it.

'It'll take hours for you to get the machinery in place, much less start digging,' Em told them. 'Sam's growing quieter by the minute. He's in shock. He needs a drip to keep his blood pressure up, he needs pain relief and, above all else, he needs someone near him. You tell me there's a slight ledge beside his head where the wall's moved…'

'We don't know how stable it is.'

'I won't put weight on it. I'll just use it to lever myself into position. If you can harness me, I'll be held from above and all my weight can stay on the harness. I'll wear a hard hat and I'll take another down for Sam.' She looked around at the group of strained faces. 'Please,' she said. 'It's the only hope he has of surviving.'

They didn't like it. They didn't like it one bit. But they measured the width of the narrow part of the shaft. It'd fit Em's shoulders with an inch to spare.

And it wouldn't fit anyone else but a child.

'There you go, then,' Em told them. 'It finally pays to be skinny. So rig me up and get me down there.'

'Em…' It was Jonas, and his face was etched harshly with strain. 'The shaft—it's moved already with the land-slip. God knows how stable it is. Hell, you can't—'

She couldn't get emotional. 'Do you have any other ideas, Dr Lunn?'

'You realise the whole thing could collapse?'

'Yeah, that's just what Anna wants to hear,' she snapped. 'And me, too. So forget it. It's not going to happen. If you lower me down so slowly I'm hardly moving, I'll keep my hands away from the walls and I'll put no pressure on anything. I'm not adding to that risk very much at all.'

'You're putting two lives in danger instead of one.'

'Then dig fast,' she told him calmly, much more calmly than, in fact, she was feeling. 'And rescue both of us.'

'Oh, Em.' Anna was clutching Matt for mutual comfort, but she put her little boy down and came forward to give her doctor a hug. 'If you'd really do this for us…'

Em hugged her back. And then she stepped away, and looked to Jim. She needed to move fast here before she lost her courage.

She really wasn't *that* brave!

'I need equipment,' she told the men. 'Can you orga-nise a line so we can hoist things up and down to me? Medical equipment. Food and water if I want it. Whatever I need.'

'We can do that.' It was Jonas, and she had the overriding impression that he was close to tears. 'Em, you realise it could be tomorrow before we get Sam out. You'll be down there until then. We daren't risk pulling you up and down again.'

'Once I'm down, I'm down to stay,' she agreed, 'so let's get this right first off.'

'Em...'

'What?'

Nothing. He stared at her for a long, long minute, while all the impossibilities crowded in on him.

But there was no choice and he knew it. Without Em, they'd surely lose Sam.

But maybe they'd lose both of them.

He couldn't bear it, and his face showed that to her, too. If he could have cut off his shoulders to do this himself, he would have, she realised, and the thought inexplicably warmed her.

But she was the only one who would fit, and he was forced to let her go.

'Em,' he said again, and there was a whole depth of meaning—of longing, of fear and of love—behind his words. 'Love...'

And he took the two steps toward her. There was no choice about what he did then either.

He took her into his arms and he kissed her.

And then, after a contact so precious neither of them could realise just what it meant, he put her away from him, like a man preparing himself for a nightmare worse than anyone could imagine.

'Stay safe,' he whispered, and Em knew right then and there that his words were a plea for himself—not for her.

* * *

What followed *was* a nightmare.

Em's descent was prepared with as much care as the men could possibly muster. They planked the entire top of the shaft, fitting a net to catch any rubble before it fell. Then they widened the entrance so it was large enough to fit Em, and also so it was dead centre of the narrow gap fifteen feet down.

'Because you have to drop straight down,' she was told. 'You mustn't sway. We can rig the harness so you drop vertically and then we can pull the harness up so you're in a sitting position once you're there, but you have to slip through that gap without touching the sides. If you can't do that, you risk dislodging…'

There was no need to tell her more. She knew what she risked.

So finally, hard-hatted and overalled, placed in a harness that spread her weight through her entire body and wearing a carefully packed medical pouch around her midriff, she was gently lowered through the hole.

The last thing she remembered seeing as she looked up at the people surrounding her was Jonas.

And his face was desperate.

'Sam…'

The little boy was barely conscious. Em had been whispering to him as she descended, focusing on not touching the walls but also intent on not frightening the child into jerking when he realised she was there. He hadn't responded. Now, though, she was within inches of him.

There was a ledge—about ten inches wide or so—on either side of his head. Em shone her torch down to see how Sam was held, and her heart sank.

How had he not slipped through? He was so far through now. One more slip…

There was his head, his hair still bright red and curly, but that was about all that was recognisably Sam. He'd scratched himself falling. His face was bloody and tear-stained, and as white as death.

'Sam.'

His sightless eyes suddenly focused. He couldn't look up but, seated in her harness above him, Em's hand was on his head, gently running her fingers through his curls. Her voice was urgent.

'Sam, even though I'm here now, you're not to move an inch. In case you fall further. You understand, Sam?'

'I…' He gulped. 'Yes.' He was brave to the core. 'I understand.'

'But at least I'm here. I won't leave you.'

'Mum. Uncle Jonas,' he whispered. 'I want them.'

'I want them, too.' She forced herself to chuckle, and it echoed strangely in the darkness. 'But they're both too fat to come down.'

It was a terrifying experience, trying to hold herself still in the harness and talking into the dark. She had a flood-light on her cap, and the beam of light swung wildly as she looked about her. There was another small torch in her hand which she used to carefully examine Sam. 'You have got yourself into a pickle, haven't you.'

'I'm…I'm scared.'

'You and me both,' Em said solidly. There was no use pretending. Sam was too intelligent a kid not to pick up on a lie when he heard it. 'But we're in this together, so let's make the best of it.'

The best case scenario—the one they'd hoped against hope for when they'd lowered Em—was that somehow she could rig a harness around Sam so that he could be winched up.

It wasn't remotely possible.

One arm was out of sight. The other hand had been forced up and was wedged at an odd angle between his shoulder and the wall. Em could see his wrist and hand but that was all. The extra width of his arm was what was wedging him. If he moved that hand…

He couldn't. She was almost scared to touch him, much less try and gain a hold. She knew disaster would result.

They just had to play a waiting game.

If he started to slip, she told herself, she'd just grab him around the neck and that one hand and pull. She risked breaking his neck by doing so, but if he was going to fall it was the only chance he had.

Please, let him not slip.

'Is this the arm that hurts?' she asked, and touched his fingers with a feather touch.

'Yes. It hurts so much. It just jabs and jabs.' She didn't need to examine him to know it was true. She could hear the agony in his voice.

'I can help that.' She forced her voice to be as matter-of-fact as possible. 'Sam, I'm going to pop an injection into your neck. A pinprick—that's all. It'll make you feel really sleepy, but that's OK. You can go to sleep if you want. The men are going to dig down to reach us and it'll take ages so it's better if you sleep. And the injection will stop the pain really fast. Do you think you can hold very, very still and not even wiggle when you feel the needle?'

'I…I'll try.'

'Good kid.'

Great kid.

Please, let him not fall…

*   *   *

Em wished she could sleep herself.

Hour upon hour she waited. Sam slept and stirred and she comforted him. Over and over.

Once she knew she could reach his wrist, she called up to Jonas and he sent down what she needed to set up a saline drip. Somehow, and afterwards she could never figure out how, she inserted a needle into one of the little boy's crushed arms, then hung the saline bag on the pouch at her midriff.

Please, let him not have any internal injuries, she prayed over and over again. His pulse was thready but that might be shock.

She hung on in the dark and there was no answer to her pleas.

If Jonas hadn't been right there above her, she would have gone quietly crazy.

He talked to her. Over and over. He lay on the planking above her head and he talked her through every stage of what was happening. How they'd decided against drills because of the fear of vibrations in the unstable soil. How they were digging by hand—teams of men—every able-bodied man in the district seemed to be here now, taking turns to dig, to heave soil to the surface, to shore the new shaft, to chop timber for shoring...

It seemed everyone in Bay Beach was here. Lori. Shanni. Erin. Wendy. All her friends. They took it in turns to talk to her—Lori had even brought Bernard, for heaven's sake, and she described him as frantic. Bernard? Frantic?

'Well, he's scratching his butt,' Lori told her. 'In Bernard-speak, that's frantic.'

She smiled, but she couldn't smile for long.

But always there was Jonas, speaking softly over everyone else.

'Em, here's Lori to talk to you. With your weird dog. And Nick. Nick's been digging—you ever seen a magistrate with mud on his face? Em, Ray's been here, demanding to dig. How many weeks after a bypass? I reckon he's crazier than you are. I've told him he has to wait until you come up because I need another doctor if he's going into cardiac arrest again...'

And sometimes there was just Jonas.

'Em, I'm still here. We're all still here. We won't leave you.'

And then an even shorter message as the night grew longer and the darkness deepened. Over and over.

'I won't leave you.'

And then... 'Em, I'll never leave you.'

The discomfort was unbelievable. Em hung in her harness and kept her increasingly desperate vigil. Her hand ran through the little boy's hair over and over again, the only contact with him that she dared.

It had been almost impossible to put in the saline drip. He'd jerked once and it had scared the life out of her. So now she monitored the drip, gave him pain relief as he needed it and kept in contact with him by touching his curls.

She was starting to need the contact with Sam as much as he needed it from her.

The walls were closing in on her.

As night fell, the light from the top of the shaft dimmed and died. The shaft seemed to close in still further.

'Jonas,' she whispered, and he was there. Of course he was there. He'd promised.

'We're down fifteen feet,' he told her. 'We're moving faster than I thought possible. We'll have you out by dawn, Em.'

She took a deep breath. 'I need some light.'

'You have your flashlight. Are the batteries dying?'

'No… I mean up there. So I can see…you.'

Her voice trailed off but he had it in one. Claustrophobia was impossible to predict, and when it happened it was almost impossible to control.

'Do you need to come up?' His voice was harsh with anxiety.

'No!' No way. She couldn't leave Sam. Firstly, to drag her up past that narrow passage would risk debris falling down on him, and to come down again would be impossible.

Her claustrophobia was something she had to control all by herself—and she *had* to control it.

'I just need to see…the top,' she said.

'You will.' And then Jonas's voice rang out, curt with command, and there were suddenly floodlights playing over the top of the shaft. She could look up and see his face—his smile. He was shining the torch over his face so that he was no longer in the shadows, and she could see him clearly, even though he was so far away.

'It won't be long, Em,' he told her, his voice willing it to be the truth. 'We're boarding up the new shaft as we go, and that's what's taking the time. We can't move too fast or we risk a tragedy, but we're going as fast as humanly possible.'

Twenty feet…

She could hear them—muffled shouts, swearing, snapping commands from the top.

Twenty-five feet, Jonas told her.

Thirty feet.

And then, finally, she heard faint, muffled and far-away

noises through the dirt and rock by her side, and she knew they'd reached her level.

Still they didn't come near. They were digging a good ten feet away from the side of her shaft. They would go deeper and then across.

'It'll take two more hours,' Jonas said, and his voice was filled with confidence. It demanded confidence in return. 'Can you hold on that long, Em?'

What could she give him but confidence in return?

'Of course I can.'

At last, blessedly, there was the sound of scraping, and falling dirt, and a chink of light played *up* from under Sam's chin. Someone was *under* him.

Em had gone past discomfort. Every muscle in her body had reacted at some time and now she was cramping and tired and desperate to go to the bathroom—but Sam was shifting and *he mustn't move yet*.

'No,' she said sharply, and her hand held his hair, and stroked down to his chin. 'The men have reached under us but they don't have the planking in place yet to stop you falling. It's still not safe for us to move, Sam, love. Can you hold on for a little more?'

He was drifting in and out of consciousness, but Em didn't know how much of that was due to shock, how much to internal injuries and how much to the pain relief she'd given him. It'd have to be a combination. But what sort of combination?

Hurry...

'They're coming,' she told the little boy. 'They're very near. You'll soon be with your mum.'

As for Em, she knew what she was aching for.

She'd soon be with Jonas.

*   *   *

'Got him.'

It was a shout of triumph and it came directly from underneath Sam. To Em's astonished delight, Sam's body was raised—not much, but a fraction as his weight was taken into someone's arms from underneath, just enough for the man on the platform under him to chip away at the rocks wedging him fast.

Finally, Sam's shoulders released their grip on the rock, but instead of plunging a hundred and fifty feet he was lifted gently into the waiting arms of the man who'd released him.

As the shaft was unblocked below her harness, Em was left staring down in incredulity at the laughing, blackened face of an unknown man, jubilant with triumph.

'Is it OK if we take your patient, Doc?' he asked. He hugged Sam to him, careful not to hold him any tighter than he needed, and reached up to take the saline bag from Em. He looped the IV line carefully so the whole arrangement was resting on Sam's middle.

And that was it. 'Come on, young man. We've made this shaft wide enough to get you out.'

With that, Sam was tenderly manoeuvred out through the side shaft, out of Em's sight, and there was nothing left but for Em to be raised to the surface.

To Jonas.

Jonas suffered the diggers to help haul her to the surface, but that was all they were allowed to do. As she emerged into the breaking dawn light, it was Jonas who stepped forward and gathered her into his arms.

And he held her as if he'd never let her go again.

Ever.

CHAPTER ELEVEN

EM WOKE to the sound of the sea.

The hospital was built on a bluff overlooking the town and her bedroom faced the beach, just as it had at her grandpa's when she was a child. Which was how she was feeling right now—like a child—as if all the adulthood had been shaken right out of her.

She lay there, still and silent, letting the events of the past twenty-four hours soak into her consciousness. Slowly. Taking it step by step, for fear of being overwhelmed.

There'd been the dread. The terror that Sam would fall, the fear that she couldn't bear her own physical discomfort and the unexpected claustrophobia on top of it.

And then there'd been the relief of tension that had been so great that, on reaching the surface, she'd wept and wept, like an inconsolable child instead of a mature, dedicated doctor. So much so that after Jonas had made sure Sam was OK, he'd turned to her and ordered tranquillisers and bed, and he'd brooked no argument.

He'd wanted to carry her home himself. She'd seen that. But Sam had been his greatest need, and Em had pulled herself together enough to tell him to get his priorities right. As he had to. Chris, the doctor from down south, had arrived so, thank God, she hadn't been needed to assist medically.

Which was just as well. She couldn't have fought her way out of a paper bag, much less assist in treating Sam.

So here she was, alone in her own safe bed, and suddenly she was grateful for that loneliness. There were so many things crowding in on her—things she needed time to come to terms with.

Ghosts, she thought, suddenly—irrelevantly. With the sounds of the sea came the whispering echoes of the past—Grandpa and Charlie. They'd taught her to love the sea. They'd taught her to love Bay Beach, so much that she'd dedicated her life to being its doctor.

And now a tremulous hope was building and building that maybe the sacrifices she'd made were no longer necessary.

Jonas... What had he said?

'I'll never leave you...'

It was just something he'd said to allay her fears, she told herself shakenly. It had been said in the urgency of the moment.

It had been for comfort. Not the truth.

Robby... Think of Robby. She should get up and check on her baby.

Why wasn't he here? Beside her? She glanced at her watch and blinked her surprise. Eight a.m. It looked like early morning outside, but it couldn't be...

It was. She'd slept the clock around and then some.

But no one was here to verify it. Not even Bernard the dog. There was only the sound of the sea for company, but the need for solitude was over.

She needed more. Just as she put a hand on her covers, the door opened—and it was Jonas.

But this was a different Jonas. This was a Jonas she'd never seen before. He looked lighter, she thought. Younger. He looked like a man who'd had the weight of the world taken from his shoulders. His burnt red hair was bright in the morning sunshine, his green eyes twinkled, he looked clean and groomed and a thousand miles from the distraught man she'd seen the day before.

Her Jonas…

He peeped around her bedroom door, and his smile as he saw that she was awake broadened into a full-sized grin. Then, before she could say a word, he was across the room and she'd been taken firmly into his arms.

'My Em.'

He held her close, his chest crushing her breast, and it was the action of a man who was claiming his own.

His heart.

She was dreaming. Wasn't she?

She must be. *'My Em…'* It was a dreamy whisper, wafting round and round the room, and the echo and its uncertainty made Em pull away.

That made her know she was awake. Heavens, she hurt. Every muscle in her body screamed in protest. Hanging in harness in the one position for so many hours had caused more bruising than she would have believed possible. She'd also hit the sides of the shaft on the way up.

Jonas had seen the wince and frowned swiftly in concern.

'What is it? Something I missed? Em…'

He'd examined her as she'd emerged from the shaft, she remembered, but only just. She remembered his hands running over her body as she'd sagged in his arms, checking, making sure she hadn't crashed too hard against the wall on the ascent which had proved more difficult than the descent.

She'd swayed—she hadn't been able to stop herself swaying when the urgency not to had been removed—and she'd hit the shaft sides over and over again. But to wait until they'd widened the gap where Sam had stuck so she could be lowered further and go out by the same route would have taken longer than she could stand.

No matter. She smiled her reassurance, and if her smile was wider than reassurance deserved, she couldn't help it. This was only bruising. What was at stake here was far more important. What had he called her? *'My Em…'*

'I'm fine,' she lied, and looked up at Jonas though a dreamy mist. 'What did you say?'

His gaze narrowed, and he looked confused. '"What is it?"'

'No.' She was onto something important here, and she was holding on to it like a pit bull terrier. 'Before that.'

'Before that?'

'You said "my Em".'

'So I did,' he said, and there was a touch of triumph in his voice. He pulled her against him again and kissed the top of her hair. 'I did at that. My Em.'

'Mmm.' This was definitely satisfactory. More than satisfactory.

'Your hair has dust all through it,' he said softly, kissing the top of her head. 'I really, really need to unbraid it.'

'You can chop it off for all I care.'

'Emily!' His voice was shocked, but filled with laughter. 'Sacrilege.' There was also something else in his voice, Em noticed.

Love?

And it was. He cupped her chin in his hands, and he looked deep into her eyes. 'You know I want to marry you?' he said tenderly. 'You know that, don't you, love?'

Her heart almost stopped, right there and then.

'But you said that before,' she whispered. 'That you wanted to marry me.'

'Yeah, but for all the wrong reasons.'

'So you have some new ones?'

'Let's say I had 'em all along—I was just too stupid to see them. I wanted to marry you because I thought you and Robby needed me. And that was fine. What I was too stupid to realise was that I needed you far, far more.'

'I...I see.'

'Poor love, you're still half-exhausted. It's not fair to spring this on you now.' But all the same, his hand went to the knot at the base of her braid. He slipped off the band holding it secure and then very, very slowly he started unbraiding.

The feeling was incredible. It was so sensual it made Em want to cry out with pleasure.

Or take him into her arms and...

'You know Sam's fine?' he said, and she blinked.

'What? Oh, Sam. Yes.' She nodded. She'd made sure of that before she'd let anyone give her any pills. He was one tough little boy.

'He has one badly broken arm, which Chris and I set last night. He also has massive bruising and a fair few abrasions, but as far as we can see the damage is external only. He's also suffering from shock. He's asleep at the moment. Anna is with him. She slept in the hospital beside him, and she's still there now.'

'Anna...' That stirred her. She glanced at her watch. Anna had so much on her plate. For heaven's sake, wasn't this the day...? 'Anna was supposed to start radiotherapy today,' she managed. 'Did someone remember to cancel for her?'

'Ever the doctor.' Jonas was laughing at her. His hand was halfway up the braid now, moving through her silky tresses with the tenderness of a lover. 'Actually we've put radiotherapy off for a while. For three months, in fact.

Quite a lot has happened while you've been sleeping, my love.'

My love. Em liked that. She definitely liked it. But she still had to concentrate on Anna. 'Why?' she managed, and it was all she could do not to shudder with pleasure as his hands reached her shoulders.

'Because Anna has decided to have chemotherapy first.

That reached her. She pushed Jonas away and stared. 'I don't understand,' she said, and he shook his head and smiled at her. And his smile was a caress all by itself.

'I'm not sure I do either, completely,' he told her. 'I only know that Anna and Jim carried Sam into the hospital together, they're still sitting side by side, hand in hand, there have been vows made that Anna never thought she'd make in her life, and she's elected to change her mind about chemotherapy.'

'But why?'

Jonas's smile deepened in satisfaction. 'Anna tells me she has a great chance of life now, and she wants to increase that chance to every last possibility she can get her hands on of living to a hundred. Even if it means depending on the whole town. Because…'

Jonas's voice broke with emotion. His hands came out and caught hers, and he forced himself to continue. 'Because, like me, she's realised that dependence cuts both ways. She saw Jim's face while he fought for her son's life. She knows how much he cares for her kids as well as for her, and she wants that love very much.'

'So much that she'll give up her independence to have it?'

'Independence isn't all it's cracked up to be,' Jonas said carefully. 'For me and Anna both. Like Anna, I've been working on it for a long time now, and suddenly I figure it's not that great.'

'Because?' Em could scarcely breathe.

'Because it doesn't work,' he said roughly, and the strain of the past hours told in his voice. 'Oh, sure, I was happy for Anna to depend on me—for you and Robby and even Bernard the dog to depend on me—and then when you were down that damned shaft I realised that if you were lost…'

'Hush,' she said softly as his voice cracked, and her hand went up to rake those beloved curls. 'Hush.'

'No.' He broke away and looked at her. 'I need to say it. Em, nothing could be worse than losing you. *Nothing*. I've tried to keep my independence and I've failed. First I told myself it was just that I'd fallen for Robby—that it was one courageous baby I was working for. He needed me and Robby was the reason I offered marriage. But then there was you.'

'Jonas—'

He was brooking no interruption. 'And I could see that his mother needed me, too. Only then she dared to say she loved me, and that threatened my independence. It was all right to be needed, but not to be loved.'

'I don't—'

'You don't understand because you've never needed to.' His hand went back to her hair and the final few twists were unbraided. In triumph he splayed it out over his fingers, the gorgeous dark curls slipping through his hands over and over again. 'You've known all along what it is to love, and you do it. You give and you give. You love this town. Its people. You love Robby. You even love that misbegotten floormat you call Bernard who, by the way, is having a rollicking good time with Lori and Matt and Ruby. He's not faithful in the least. Whereas I…'

'Whereas you…?' Joy was building in Em—a joy so great that her world felt it was exploding into a million multicoloured shards. Here, then, was the happy ending she'd never dreamed of finding.

Or the happy beginning.

'Whereas I intend to be faithful—to you and to our Robby and to Bernard and whoever else just happens to come along—' his eyes glinted down at her with dangerous laughter '—for a very long time.' Then he pulled her into his arms and held her with such tenderness she wanted to weep.

But she couldn't, because he was cupping her face, he was lifting her mouth to be kissed, and he was kissing her for ever.

Not quite for ever.

Jonas pulled away—at last—and his voice was a hoarse whisper of passion.

'How about sixty years of marriage?' he said at last. 'Bare minimum. Sixty years of happy-ever-after. Let's work on that, my love, and then, when we've achieved it, we'll see if we can do better than even Anna and Jim intend to do.'

And it sounded OK to Emily.

In fact, it sounded just fine!

EPILOGUE

ROBBY became Robby Lunn ten months later, and the whole of Bay Beach turned out to celebrate. Well, why not? Robby was one special little boy. Jonas and Em, his adoptive parents, were also deemed very special people, and the residents of Bay Beach decided this adoption was worthy of their best celebratory efforts.

Even Robby's aunt was smiling. As well she should. Everyone approved her actions here. To give her nephew a home with Jonas and Em was just fine. The town just had to look at them to know they'd make wonderful parents. They had love to spare, and there'd be no criticism at all of her decision to allow the adoption to go through.

So there was only approval here today—approval from everyone.

Tom Burrows was here—as head of the orphanage service, he was beaming as if he'd personally organised the whole thing.

The Bay Beach Orphanage service wasn't just represented by Tom. The house mothers or ex-house mothers were out in force. Shanni and Nick were here surrounded by their tribe of children. Wendy and Luke had a happy little Gabbi tucked by their side, and there was an addition to the family on the way there, too.

Matt and Erin had their terrible twins in check. Just. And Lori was here, holding hands with Ray and surrounded by their five foster-kids.

Marriage to Lori meant that Ray was now a house parent himself, a role he'd taken on on the basis that if he couldn't beat them he'd join them. He'd slimmed right down. Caring for five children was the best heart's cure Emily could think of, and it had worked a treat.

And Anna and Jim were there. Of course they were, and it was a newly married Anna who was facing a new beginning.

She was looking lovely. She was wearing a gorgeous, soft auburn wig, and despite the responsibility of her three youngsters—tumbling on the lawn with Bernard-the-dog and Erin's and Matt's twins—Anna looked young and carefree and indescribably pretty. She'd come through her treatment with flying colours, she'd finally let go of the steely independence she'd held onto for so long, she'd reached out to Jim—and to Jonas—and she was looking happier now than Em had ever seen her.

As was Em.

Em stood in the garden by Jonas's side while the formal signing for adoption took place, and she smiled and she smiled and she smiled.

All these people she loved so much...

Her wedding day had been wonderful but today was even better. Today she stood by her husband's side. Jonas was holding her beloved Robby in his arms with a look that said he'd never let him go, and her heart was threatening to burst.

And there was more. Tonight, she thought. Tonight she'd confess to Jonas that this was just the beginning. Inside her womb a tiny seed was starting to grow. She'd done a pregnancy test that morning, and the magic was all about her.

'Happy?' That was Jonas, whispering down to her as the photographer lined them up for their first ever formal family portrait.

Happy? How could she not be happy?

'Fit to bust,' she said inelegantly, and he chuckled, put his arm around his wife's waist and pulled her into him.

'I don't know about this formal photograph business,' he told her. 'How will we explain to our grandchildren that Grandpa didn't always wear his hair like this?'

'You might not have any by the time you have grandkids,' she told him cheerfully. He'd shaved his hair when Anna had lost hers—as he'd said he would—and he'd kept it off until Anna had confided that hers was growing back under the wig, but his hair was still very, very short. 'When you're a grandpa you might be balder than Anna ever was!'

'Good grief!' He hadn't thought of that. He put his wife away from him and looked at her with mock anxiety. 'What if I am? You've loved me once when I was bald, my darling Em. Do you think you can love me again?'

'I won't have to,' she said serenely, and she lifted a chortling Robby from her husband's arms and gave him a squeeze—because if she didn't squeeze someone she'd burst with happiness.

'Why not?'

'Because to love again means I have to stop and start again,' she told him. 'And I don't think I can do that.'

'No?' He was making love to her with his eyes, and his smile was warming her through and through.

'It seems Bay Beach isn't the place to stop loving,' she told him, her voice alight with love and laughter. Robby gave her arm a tug, she set him down on his sturdy little legs and watched him waddle off Bernard-wards. Then, unable to contain herself any longer, she let herself be caught in her husband's arms and held. For a very long time.

'Look about you,' she whispered. 'All of us... We're

all happy-ever-afters if I ever saw them. Bay Beach is a place of miracles, Jonas Lunn.'

'Just one miracle,' Jonas said thickly, pulling her into him so she was crushed against his heart. 'Just one miracle, my love. And that miracle is you.'

And who was Emily to disagree with that?

eHARLEQUIN.com

community | membership

buy books | authors | online reads | magazine | learn to write

magazine

♥ ——————————————— **quizzes**

Is he the one? What kind of lover are you? Visit the **Quizzes** area to find out!

♥ ——————————————— **recipes for romance**

Get scrumptious meal ideas with our **Recipes for Romance**.

♥ ——————————————— **romantic movies**

Peek at the **Romantic Movies** area to find Top 10 Flicks about First Love, ten Supersexy Movies, and more.

♥ ——————————————— **royal romance**

Get the latest scoop on your favorite royals in **Royal Romance**.

♥ ——————————————— **games**

Check out the **Games** pages to find a ton of interactive romantic fun!

♥ ——————————————— **romantic travel**

In need of a romantic rendezvous? Visit the **Romantic Travel** section for articles and guides.

♥ ——————————————— **lovescopes**

Are you two compatible? Click your way to the **Lovescopes** area to find out now!

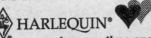

HARLEQUIN® ♥

makes any time special—online...

Visit us online at
www.eHarlequin.com

If you enjoyed what you just read,
then we've got an offer you can't resist!

Take 2 bestselling love stories FREE!

Plus get a FREE surprise gift!

MONTANA
Bred

From the bestselling series

MONTANA MAVERICKS

Wed in Whitehorn

Two more tales that capture living and loving
beneath the Big Sky.

JUST PRETENDING by Myrna Mackenzie

FBI Agent David Hannon's plans for a quiet vacation
were overturned by a murder investigation—and by
officer Gretchen Neal!

STORMING WHITEHORN by Christine Scott

Native American Storm Hunter's return to Whitehorn
sent tremors through the town—and shock waves of
desire through Jasmine Kincaid Monroe....

Silhouette ®

Where love comes alive ™

Visit Silhouette at www.eHarlequin.com

PSBRED

Liz Fielding

**Winner of the 2001 RITA Award for
Best Traditional Romance, awarded for**

THE BEST MAN
AND THE BRIDESMAID

Coming soon:
an emotionally thrilling new trilogy from this
award-winning Harlequin Romance® author:

It's a marriage takeover!

Claibourne & Farraday is an exclusive London department
store run by the beautiful Claibourne sisters, Romana, Flora
and India. But their positions are in jeopardy—the seriously
attractive Farraday men want the store back!

It's an explosive combination...but with a little bit of
charm, passion and power these gorgeous men become
BOARDROOM BRIDEGROOMS!

Look out in Harlequin Romance® for:

May 2002
THE CORPORATE BRIDEGROOM (#3700)

June 2002
THE MARRIAGE MERGER (#3704)

July 2002
THE TYCOON'S TAKEOVER (#3708)

Available wherever Harlequin® books are sold.

HARLEQUIN®
*M*akes any time special ®

Visit us at www.eHarlequin.com